keeping the moon

Sarah Dessen

PUFFIN BOOKS

PUFFIN BOOKS

Published by the Penguin Group

Penguin Putnam Books for Young Readers,

345 Hudson Street, New York, New York 10014, U.S.A.

Penguin Books Ltd, 27 Wrights Lane, London W8 5TZ, England

Penguin Books Australia Ltd, Ringwood, Victoria, Australia

Penguin Books Canada Ltd, 10 Alcorn Avenue, Toronto, Ontario, Canada M4V 3B2

Penguin Books (N.Z.) Ltd, 182-190 Wairau Road, Auckland 10, New Zealand

Penguin Books Ltd, Registered Offices: Harmondsworth, Middlesex, England

First published by Viking, a division of Penguin Putnam Books for Young Readers, 1999

Published by Puffin Books, a division of Penguin Putnam Books for Young Readers, 2000

7 9 10 8

THE LIBRARY OF CONGRESS HAS CATALOGED THE VIKING EDITION AS FOLLOWS

Dessen, Sarah.

Keeping the moon/Sarah Dessen.

p. cm.

Summary: Fifteen-year-old Colie, a former fat girl, spends the summer working
as a waitress in a beachside restaurant, staying with her overweight and
eccentric Aunt Mira, and trying to explore her sense of self

ISBN 0-670-88549-5

[1. Self-esteem Fiction. 2. Weight control Fiction. 3. Restaurants Fiction
4. Aunts Fiction.] I. Title.

PZ7.D455Ke 1999 [Fic]—dc21 99-19597 CIP

Puffin ISBN 0-14-131007-3

Printed in the United States of America

For Lee Smith, who taught me
and for past and present dancing burritogirls everywhere

I would like to acknowledge Janet Marks
and the Hensley family for their unwavering presence
and support, and Phil and Vicki Campbell for my years at
the Flying Burrito—the inspiration for this story and
countless others. Thank you.

chapter one

My name is Nicole Sparks. Welcome to the first day of the worst summer of my life.

"Colie," my mother said with a sigh as she walked down the train platform toward me. She was in one of her FlyKiki workout suits, purple this time; she looked like a shiny grape. Her assistant, standing by the station door, took a not-so-subtle look at her watch. "Will you please try not to look so tortured?"

I fake-smiled at her, crossing my arms more tightly over my chest.

"Oh, that's even worse," she said. Another sigh. "With your hair that color and that thing in your lip you look terrible even when you're smiling." She came closer, her sneakers making squeaky mouse noises on the concrete. Like everything else, they were brand-new. "Honey, you know this is for the best.

You couldn't stay by yourself at the house all summer. You'd be lonely."

"I have friends, Mom," I said.

She cocked her head to the side, as if she doubted this. "Oh, honey," she said again. "It's for the best."

The best for you, I thought. The thing about my mother is that she always has good intentions. But that's as far as she usually gets.

"Kiki," said the assistant, whose name I hadn't even bothered to learn because she'd be gone by the time I got back, fired before they even reached the airport, probably, "we've got to go if we want to make that flight."

"All right, all right." My mother put her hands on her hips—the classic Kiki Sparks aerobic stance—and looked me up and down. "You'll keep up your workouts, right? It would be a shame to gain all that weight back."

"Yes."

"And you'll eat healthy—I told you I'm sending along the complete Kiki line—so you'll have your foods with you at Mira's."

"You told me."

She let her hands drop to her sides, and in that one brief moment I saw my mother again. Not Kiki Sparks, fitness guru and personal trainer of the masses. Not the talk show Kiki, the infomercial Kiki, the Kiki that smiled out from a million weight-loss products worldwide. Just my mom.

But now the train was coming.

"Oh, Colie," she said, and she pulled me close, burying her face in the jet-black hair that had almost made her have a total

TURN THE PAGE FOR A SPECIAL PREVIEW OF SARAH DESSEN'S NEW NOVEL,

DREAMLAND

Caitlin doesn't want to leave dreamland, a half-sleeping state where she can keep everything—and everyone—at arm's length. If she left, she'd have to deal with her sister's sudden absence, her mother's inattentiveness, and her new boyfriend's dangerous dark side.

In her most compelling and challenging novel yet, acclaimed author Sarah Dessen tells the story of Caitlin's harrowing journey through a nightmarish dreamland, and of her potent and affecting awakening.

My sister Cass ran away the morning of my sixteenth birthday. She left my present, wrapped and sitting outside my bedroom door, and stuck a note for my parents under the coffeemaker. None of us heard her leave.

I was dreaming when I woke up suddenly to the sound of my mother screaming. I ran to my door, threw it open, and promptly tripped over my gift, whacking my face on a hall light switch. My face was aching as I got to my feet and ran down the hall to the kitchen, where my mother was standing by the coffeemaker with Cass's note in her hand.

"I just don't *understand* this," she was saying shakily to my father, who was standing beside her in his pajamas without his glasses on. The coffeemaker was spitting and gurgling happily behind them, like this was any other morning. "She can't just leave. She *can't.*"

"Let me see the note," my father said calmly, taking it out of her hand. It was on Cass's thick, monogrammed stationery with matching envelopes. I had the same ones, same initials: CO.

Later, when I read it, I saw it was completely concise and to the point. Cass was not the type to waste words.

Mom and Dad,

> *I want you to know, first, that I'm sorry about this. Someday I hope I'll be able to explain it well enough so that you'll understand.*

> *Please don't worry. I'll be in touch.*

> *I love you both.*

Cass

My mother wiped her eyes with the back of her hand and looked at me. "She's gone," she said. "She went to be with *him*, I know it. How can she do this? She's supposed to be at Yale in two weeks."

"Margaret," my father said, squinting at the note. "Calm down."

The "him" was Cass's boyfriend, Adam: He was twenty-one, had a goatee, and lived in New York working on the *Lamont Whipper Show*. It was one of those shock talk shows where people tell their boyfriends they've been sleeping with their best friends and guests routinely include Klansmen and eighty-pound four-year-olds. Adam's job mostly consisted of getting coffee, picking up people at the airport, and pulling guests off each other during the frequent fights that scored the show big ratings. Since she'd come home from the beach three weeks ago—she'd met Adam there—Cass had been glued to the TV each day at 4 P.M., wishing aloud for a good fight just so she could catch a glimpse of him. Usually she did, smiling at the sight of him charging onstage, his face serious, to untangle two scrapping sisters or a couple of rowdy cross-dressers.

My father put the note down on the table and walked to the phone. "I'm calling the police," he said, and my mother burst into tears again, her hands rising to her face. Over her shoulder, through the glass door and over the patio, I could see our neighbors, Boo and Stewart Connell. They were cutting through the tree line that separated our houses for my birthday brunch; Boo had a bouquet of fresh-cut zinnias, bright and colorful, in her hand.

"I just can't believe this," my mother said to me, pulling out a chair and sitting down at the table. She was shaking her head. "What if something happens to her? She's only eighteen."

"Yes, hello, I'm calling to report a missing person," my father said suddenly, in his official Dean of Students voice. "Cassandra O'Koren. Yes. She's my daughter."

I had a sudden memory pop into my head: my mother, standing in the doorway of Cass's and my childhood room, back when we had twin beds and pink wallpaper. She would always kiss us, then stand in the doorway after turning off the light, her shadow stretching down the length of the room between us. She was always the last thing I tried to see before I fell asleep.

"See you in dreamland," she'd whisper, and blow us a kiss before shutting the door quietly behind her. Like dreamland was a real place, tangible, where we would all wander close enough to catch glimpses and brush shoulders. I always went to sleep determined to go there, to find her and Cass, and sometimes I did. But it was never the way I imagined it would be.

Now my mother sat weeping as my father reported Cass's vital statistics—five-four, brown hair, brown eyes, mole on left cheek—and I had the sudden sinking feeling that dreamland might be the only place we'd be seeing her for a while.

I heard a knock and looked up to see Boo and Stewart standing on the patio, waving at us. They'd been our neighbors for as long as I could remember, since before Cass or I was even born. They were former hippies, now New Agers; they believed in massage, fresh-baked homemade bread, and the Dalai Lama. They had absolutely nothing in common with my parents, except proximity, which had led to eighteen years of being neighbors and our best family friends.

"Good morning!" Boo called out to us through the door, holding up the flowers for me to see. "Happy birthday!" She reached down and pushed the door open, then stepped inside with Stewart following. He was carrying a bowl and a plate, each covered with a brightly colored napkin, which he put down on the table in front of my mother.

"We brought blueberry buckwheat pancake mix and sliced mangoes," Stewart said in his soft voice, smiling at me. "Your favorites."

Boo was crossing the room, arms already extended, to pull me close for a tight, long hug. "Happy birthday, Caitlin," she whispered in my ear. She smelled like bread and incense. "This will be your best year yet. I can feel it."

"Don't count on it," I said, and she pulled back and frowned at me, confused, just as my father hung up the phone and cleared his throat.

"Technically," he said, "they can't do anything for twenty-four hours. But they're keeping an eye out for her. We need to call all her friends, right now. Maybe she told someone something."

"What's going on?" Boo asked, and at the table my mother just shook her head. She couldn't even say it. "Margaret? What is it?"

"It's Cassandra," my father told her, his voice flat. "It appears that she's run away." This was my father, always formal: He lived for *supposedlys* and *theoreticallys,* not believing anything without proper proof.

"Oh, my God," Boo said, pulling out a chair and yanking it close to my mother before sitting down. "When did she go?"

"I don't know," my mother said softly, and Boo took one of her hands, rubbing the fingers with her own, as Stewart moved to stand behind her, his hand on her shoulder. They were touchy people, always had been. My father, however, was not, so neither made a move toward him. My mother sniffled. "I don't know anything."

"Caitlin," my father said to me briskly, "get a list together of her friends, anyone she might have talked to. And the number for that Whitter show, or whatever it's called."

"Okay," I said, not bothering to correct him. He nodded before turning his back to my mother and Boo and Stewart to look out across the patio at the few squirrels crowding the bird feeders.

On my way back to my room I picked up my present from where it was lying in the middle of the hallway. It was wrapped in blue paper, with no card, but I knew it was from Cass. She would never have forgotten my birthday.

I took it into my room and sat down on my bed. In the mirror over my bureau I could see my face was scratched from where I'd hit the light switch, the skin around it a bright pink. No one had even noticed.

I unwrapped Cass's present slowly, folding the paper carefully as I slipped it off. It was a book, and as I turned it over I read the letters on the cover: *Dream Journal*. All around the words were comets and stars, moons and suns, scattered across a light purple background. It was beautiful.

The first page was an introduction about dreams, what they mean, and why we should remember them. This was Cass's thing— she had been big into symbols and signs in the last year. She said you never knew what the world was trying to tell you, that you had to pay attention every second.

As I closed the cover, something caught my eye on one of the first pages. It was an inscription in Cass's loopy script, my name big, the message little.

Caitlin, it said in black ink, *I'll see you there.*

breakdown when I came to breakfast that morning. "Please don't be mad at me. Okay?"

I hugged her back, even though I'd told myself I wouldn't. I'd pictured myself stony and silent as the train pulled out of the station, my angry face the last image she'd take with her on her European Summer FlyKiki Fitness Tour. But I was the opposite of my mother, in more than just the fact that I always had bad intentions. And that was as far as *I* got.

"I love you," she whispered as we walked toward the train.

Then take me with you, I thought, but she was already pulling back, wiping her eyes, and I knew if I said it the words would fall between us and just lie there, causing more trouble than they were worth.

"I love you too," I said. When I got to my seat I looked out the window and found her standing by the station door, her assistant still fidgeting beside her. She waved, in all that purple, and I waved back, even as the lump formed hard and throbbing in the back of my throat. Then I put on my headphones, turned up my music as loud as I could, and closed my eyes as the train slipped away.

It hadn't always been like this.

In my first real memory, at five, I am wearing white mary janes and sitting in the front seat of our old Volaré station wagon in front of a 7–Eleven. It is really, really hot, and my mother is walking toward me carrying two Big Gulps, a bag of Fritos, and a box of Twinkies. She's wearing cowboy boots, red ones, and a short skirt, even though this is during what we call the "Fat

Years." Being obese—she topped out, at her worst, at about 325 pounds—never stopped my mother from following fads.

She opens the car door and tosses in the loot, the bag of Fritos banking off my leg and onto the floor.

"Scoot over," she says, settling her large form in beside me. "We've still got half a day till Texas."

The rest of my early memories are all of highway, coming toward me from different landscapes: flat, dry desert; thick Carolina pines; windy coastal roads framed by dunes. Only a few things stayed the same. My mother and I were both fat. It was usually not too far to the next place. And we were always together, us against the world.

The last of our stops was Charlotte, North Carolina, three years ago. It's the longest I've ever stayed in any one school. It's also where my mother became Kiki Sparks.

Before, she was just Katharine, college dropout and master of a million small talents: she'd pumped gas, peddled cemetery plots over the phone, sold Mary Kay cosmetics, even arranged appointments at an escort service. Anything to keep us in food and gas money until she started itching to travel again. But after a few days in Charlotte she applied for a job at a dry cleaner's which she didn't get and, in a fit of frustration, accidentally rear-ended a Cadillac in the parking lot. Since we were flat broke, she talked the owner of the car, who ran a gym called Lady Fitness, into letting her work off the cost of the repairs. She started by cleaning the machines and answering phones, but after a few weeks the woman liked her so much she gave her a full-time job and a free membership. A week earlier we'd been back to ketchup soup and ramen noodles, sleeping in the back of the car; now, we had a steady income and a decent apartment. Back in the Fat Years, things always seemed to work out at the last minute.

My mom had been trying to lose weight all her life. At Lady Fitness, it actually started to happen. She'd always loved to dance, and she got hooked on aerobics, taking classes whenever she could fit them in. After a week or two she started dragging me with her. It was kind of embarrassing. She was *super* enthusiastic, the one voice you could hear above all the rest, all three hundred pounds of her touch-stepping and heel-toeing, clapping her hands and singing along to the music.

The instructors, however, *loved* her. After a few months one of them started helping her prepare for the certification test so she could teach her own classes. When she passed she became the heaviest—and most popular—instructor in the history of Lady Fitness. She played the best music, knew all her students by name, and used the stories of our Fat Years to emphasize her message that anyone can do *anything* they set their mind to.

By the time we'd been in Charlotte two years, my mother had lost a hundred and sixty pounds, with me shedding forty-five and a half right beside her. Katharine disappeared, along with the breakfasts of doughnuts and chocolate milk, our love handles and our double chins, and Kiki was born.

She loved her new, strong body, but for me it was harder. Even though I'd been teased all my life, I'd always taken a small, strange comfort in my folds of fat, the fact that I could grab myself at the waist. The weight was like a force field, shielding me as I was plopped into one new school after another, food being my only comfort through the long afternoons while my mother was working. Now, almost fifty pounds lighter, I had nothing left to hide behind. Sometimes in my bed at night, I'd find myself still pinching the skin at my waist, forgetting that there was nothing there to hold on to anymore.

My body had changed, parts of me just disappearing like I'd wished them away. I had cheekbones, muscles, a flat stomach, clear skin, just like my mother. But something was missing, something that made us different. I could build muscle, but not confidence. There were no exercises for that.

Still, I kept working out—doing aerobics, jogging, lifting weights—driven by the echo of words I'd been hearing for as long as I could remember.

Fat Ass! I'd force myself to do ten more lunges, feeling the burning in my legs.

Lard-O! I'd push through another set of repetitions, curling the dumbbell tight into my arm, even when the pain was killing me.

Thunder Thighs! I'd go another mile, running fast enough, finally, to leave the voices behind me.

My mother and I had become new people: even the pictures in our photo albums didn't look like us anymore. Sometimes I imagined our former fat selves were still out there driving around the country like ghosts, eating bags of Doritos. It was strange.

Meanwhile, my mom's classes at Lady Fitness kept growing, with women crowding in hip to hip to follow her gospel. Then the local cable access channel asked her to do a live morning show called *Wake Up and Work Out.* I watched her before school as I sat at the kitchen table eating my nonfat yogurt and high-energy Grape-Nuts.

"My name is Kiki Sparks," she said at the beginning of every show, while the music built behind her, louder and louder. "Are we ready to get to work?"

Soon you could almost hear the hundreds—then thousands—of women across the city shouting, "*Yes!*"

It was only a matter of time before she went statewide, then national. The woman who'd hired her at Lady Fitness mortgaged her house to produce a high-tech "FlyKiki" video, which sold a million copies after my mom appeared on the Home Shopping Network and led the host in a five-minute Super Cal Burn. The rest is fat-free history.

Now we have a house with a pool, keep a cook who makes only low-fat meals, and I have my own bathroom and TV. The only downside is that my mother is so busy, spreading Kiki-mania across the country and around the world. But whenever I miss her too much, I can flip through the channels for her infomercial—*KikiSpeaks: You Can Do It!*—and find her, just like that.

Sometimes, though, I still think about us bumping along together in our old Volaré, me half asleep with my head in her lap while she sang along with the radio. And I miss that endless highway stretching out ahead, full of possibilities, always leading to a new town and another school where I could start again.

○

When the train pulled into the Colby station five hours later, the only person waiting was a guy with shoulder-length brown hair, a tie-dyed T-shirt, cutoff army shorts, and Birkenstocks. He had about a million of those Deadhead hippie bracelets on his wrist, and he was wearing sunglasses with blue frames.

I was the only one who got off in Colby.

I stood on the platform, squinting. It was really sunny and hot, even though the ocean was supposed to be close by.

"Nicole?" the guy said, and when I looked up he took a few steps toward me. His shorts were splattered with white paint and I was sure he'd smell of patchouli or pot if I bothered to sniff hard, which I chose not to.

"Colie," I said.

"Right." He smiled. I couldn't see his eyes. "Mira sent me to pick you up. I'm Norman."

Mira was my aunt. She was stuck with me for the summer.

"Those yours?" he said, pointing at the bags, which the porter had piled further down the platform. I nodded and he started after them, with a slow, lazy walk that was already irritating me.

I was immediately mortified to see the entire Kiki line right there next to my stuff. The Kiki Buttmaster, a carton of Kiki-Eats, the dozen new FlyKiki videos and inspirational tapes, plus a few more boxes of vitamins and fitness wear with my mother's smiling face plastered across them.

"Wow," Norman said. He picked up the Buttmaster, turning it in his hands. "What's *this* for?"

"I'll get that," I said, grabbing it from him. For the entire trip down I'd imagined myself in Colby as mysterious, different; the dark stranger, answering no one's questions. This image was significantly harder to maintain while lugging a Buttmaster in front of the only boy I'd seen in the last year who didn't automatically assume I was a slut.

"Car's over here," he said, and I followed him to a battered old Ford station wagon parked in the empty lot. He put my bags in the back and held the door as I threw in the Buttmaster, which landed with a clunk on the floor. We had to make a second trip for the rest of the Kikicrap.

"So how was the train ride?" he asked. The car smelled like old leaves and was full of junk, except for the front, which had obviously been cleared out just recently. In the backseat were four mannequins, all of them headless. One was missing an arm, another a hand, but they were lined up neatly, as if they'd piled in for the ride.

"Fine," I said, wondering what kind of weirdo Mira had sent for me. I got in and slammed the door, then caught a glimpse of myself in the side mirror. In all the confusion I had forgotten about my hair. It was so black that for a second I didn't recognize myself.

Norman started up the car with a little coaxing, and we pulled out into the empty intersection.

"So," he said, "did it hurt?"

"Did what hurt?"

He looked over at me and touched the right corner of his upper lip. "That," he said. "Did it hurt, or what?"

I ran my tongue along the inside of my lip, feeling the small metal hoop there. I'd had it done only months earlier, but it felt like it had always been part of me, my touchstone. "No," I said.

"Wow," he said. The light turned green; we chugged slowly forward. "Looks like it would."

"It didn't." I said it flatly, so he wouldn't ask again.

We didn't talk as we drove. Norman's car was downright strange; besides our headless fellow passengers there were about twenty tiny plastic animals glued to the dashboard, lined up carefully, and a huge pair of fuzzy red dice bouncing from the rearview mirror.

"Nice car," I said·under my breath. He had to be some kind of art freak.

"Thanks," he replied cheerfully, reaching up to adjust a red giraffe by the air vent. He obviously thought I was serious. "It's a work in progress."

We turned on to a dirt road and passed a few houses with glimpses of water just beyond. We went all the way to the very end, finally turning in to park right in front of a big white house. Around the porch, I could see the beach and the sound. There were little boats out there, bobbing.

Norman honked the horn twice and cut the engine. "She's expecting you," he said. He got out and went around to the back door, unloading my stuff and piling it on the front steps. He put the Buttmaster on the very top, arranging it just so. I couldn't tell if he was being a smartass or what.

"Thanks," I said under my breath, deciding he was.

Mira's porch was the old southern kind: wide and long, running the entire length of the house, and I noticed two things about it right away. First, an old bicycle leaning against a front window. It had Cadillac-style fins over the back wheel and was spray-painted bright red, with a few rust spots showing through. In the metal basket on the front was a pair of sunglasses with big black frames.

The second thing I noticed was a small sign posted over the doorbell, an index card that read, in simple block letters, BELL. For the truly moronic, there was an arrow as well.

I was beginning to wonder what kind of world I had landed in.

"Norman?" A woman's voice came from inside, filtering through the screen door. "Is that you?"

"Yeah," Norman called back, walking up the steps and leaning in close against the screen, shielding his eyes with his hand. "The train was right on time, for once."

"I can't find him again," said the woman, who I assumed must be my aunt Mira. She sounded like she was moving quickly, her voice strong at first and then fading. "He was here this morning but then I just lost track of him. . . ."

"I'll look for him," Norman said, already glancing down the porch and into the yard. "He never goes far. He's probably just having issues with that dog again."

"Issues?" I said.

"Big ones," he said under his breath, still looking.

"Is Colie with you?" she said, her voice rising as she came closer.

"Yep," Norman said. "She's right here."

I kept waiting for the door to open. It didn't.

"I can't stand it when he does this," Mira said, her voice fading again. I looked at Norman, who was pacing the porch, peering over the rail to check under the house.

"We'll find him," Norman said. "Don't worry."

I just stood there. Obviously my aunt was as excited to see me as I was to come here.

I sat down next to my bag and pulled my knees to my chest. There was a rustle in the bushes, and the fattest tabby cat I'd ever seen poked his head out to look at me. He wound himself through the handrail, almost getting stuck, and brushed against me, leaving about an inch of cat hair on my black pants, jacket, and shirt. Then he climbed into my lap, clawed me for a second, and settled in.

"Cat Norman!" Norman said, and the cat turned to look at him, flicking his tail.

"What?" I said.

"Found him!" Norman yelled out.

"Did you?" said the voice from inside.

"You should take him in to her," Norman said to me. "She'll love you instantly."

"I don't like cats," I said, trying to dislodge the monster from my lap. He was purring now, a loud, rumbling noise that sounded like a chainsaw.

"Cat Norman?" Mira called out. "Come here, you terrible thing, you!"

"Take him in," Norman said again. "She's waiting." He started slowly down the steps. I noticed he moved everywhere slowly.

I stood up, the cat in my arms. He weighed about thirty pounds, as much as an entire set of KikiBell weights.

"I'll see you later," Norman said, already walking around the house, toward the backyard.

"Colie?" Mira said. Through the screen, I could almost make out a shape in the hallway. "Is he with you?"

I walked toward the door, the cat curled against me. "We're coming," I said, and I stepped inside.

The first thing I saw when my eyes adjusted was the TV in the next room. It was tuned to a wrestling match, and at that moment some huge man in a cape and a blindfold was leaping to flatten another man in purple spandex, who was writhing on the mat. As the caped man took off, his arms spread, you could see behind him rows and rows of people, aghast, as he fell fell fell toward his victim. Splat.

"Cat Norman!" my Aunt Mira said, stepping right in front of the TV and opening her arms to both of us. "And Colie. Hello!"

Mira was overweight, just like my mother had been before she became Kiki Sparks. She had a wide face and long red hair piled up on her head, like she'd done it in a hurry—a pencil and a pen were sticking out of it. She had on an old, deep green kimono patterned with dragons, a big white T-shirt, black leggings, and flip-flops. Her toenails were painted bright pink.

"Colie!" she cried again, and before I knew it she had wrapped her arms around both me and the cat. She smelled like a mix of vanilla and turpentine. "I'm so glad to see you. You look different, all grown up. And skinny! Your mom's program must work then, right?"

"Right." A piece of cat hair blew up my nose, and my eyes started watering.

"Bad, bad Cat Norman," she said to the cat, who was mashed between us, still purring. "I wonder what kind of trouble you found on *this* adventure, huh?"

The cat sneezed. Then he wriggled out of my arms, pushed off, and landed with a thud not unlike the wrestler's. He was obviously not a cat who did a lot of jumping; it was at least a second before his considerable girth caught up with him.

"Oh, you're terrible!" she scolded as he walked off, taking his time. Then she looked at me, shaking her head. "He's the light of my life, but he's in his terrible twos right now and going through a real distant phase. It's just breaking my heart."

"The cat," I said, verifying.

"Norman," she corrected me.

"Oh, Norman," I said, looking outside where I'd last seen him. "He does seem kind of spacey."

"He does?" She raised her eyebrows. "Well, it *is* summer. The heat gets to him, you know. You should see the hairballs he coughs up."

I looked back outside. "Norman does?"

"The cat," she said. "*Cat* Norman." She pointed under a chair by the door where he'd settled himself and was now licking his back leg, loudly.

"Oh," I said. "I thought you meant . . ."

"Oh, Norman," she said, and then she burst out laughing, one hand covering her mouth. She had deep dimples, like a child's. "Oh, no, not *that* Norman. I mean, he might have hairballs, with all that long hair of his. But I've never seen him coughing anything up. . . ."

"I just didn't know," I said in a low voice, and I had that sudden flash that I was fat again, could feel it on me, like I always did when someone laughed at me.

"Well," she said, linking her arm in mine, "it's an honest mistake. Cat Norman was, after all, named after Norman Norman. They are so much alike in temperament. Not to mention they both move slower than molasses."

"Norman Norman," I repeated, as we stepped into the back room. It was big and sunny and, like the porch, ran the length of the house. On the TV another match was in progress, with two small redheaded men in black trunks circling each other.

"But I need them both desperately," Mira said dramatically, glancing at the TV and then back at me. "If Norman Norman didn't live downstairs I'd have no one to open jars for me, and Cat Norman is my baby."

"Norman lives downstairs?" I said.

"Oh, yes," she said easily, sitting down in the overstuffed chair across from the television and folding the kimono neatly over her legs. On the wall was a large painting of Mira and Cat Norman sitting on the grass in front of the house. In the painting she had on a white dress and pink sunglasses shaped like stars; she was smiling. Cat Norman was beside her, his back arched as her hand brushed over him. "He stays in the downstairs room. He's no trouble. I forget he's there half the time."

As I sat down I took in the view of the ocean, the water blue and sparkling. There was a path that led down to the beach, and when I craned my neck I could see an open door and then Norman, dragging one of the headless mannequins. To the right of the path I could see a smaller house, painted the same white as Mira's. There was a clothesline beside it, with a row of brightly colored clothes flapping in the wind.

"So," she said, settling back in her chair. "How was the trip?"

"Good."

"And your mother?"

"Good."

She nodded, flashing her dimples. "Did that hurt?"

"What?"

"That thing in your lip," she said. "Ouch."

"No," I told her. "It didn't."

She nodded again. We were running out of topics. I glanced around the room. Everything was old, with a kind of tacky charm, and in need of some sort of repair: a rocking chair missing a few back slats, a small chest of drawers with faded pink paint and no knobs, a cracked fishtank full of seashells and marbles.

And then, as I looked more closely, I saw the notes. Just like the one out front, they were on index cards, written in nice block printing. WINDOW STICKS ON LEFT SIDE, it said next to the back door. CENTER LIGHT SWITCH DOES NOT WORK was posted by a switchplate on the other side of the room. And, taped to the TV set, right by the channel knob, my personal favorite: JIGGLE TO GET 11.

It was going to be a long summer.

"Oh, my!" Mira said suddenly, startling me. She lurched forward in her chair toward the television; like the cat, it took a second for everything to catch up. "Just look at that horrible El Gigantico. This isn't even his match and he's going in to attack that poor little Rex Runyon."

"What?" I said, confused.

"Look!" She pointed toward the screen. "El Gigantico's girl-friend, Lola Baby, left him for Rex Runyon last week. And now he's going to beat poor Rex to a pulp. Oh, no. Why don't the referees stop him? It's just ludicrous."

I just looked at her; she was leaning forward, eyes fixed on the screen. "Well," I said, "it *is* all—"

"Oh!" One hand flew to her mouth, her pink toes wiggling as she reacted to something on the screen. "He's pulling that figure-four move. Poor Rex. Oh, he's going to feel *that* tomorrow. I don't even know why El Gigantico cares about that Lola any-way, she's just as trashy as she can be. . . ."

"Mira," I said, "you know it's . . ." She tore her eyes away from poor Rex Runyon, who was having his head slammed into the corner of the ring, repeatedly, while the crowd counted along.

"Know it's what?" she said brightly. And I wished for a mo-ment that she had a sign too, some index card with instructions to let me know how to proceed.

"Nothing. I . . . I forgot what I was going to say," I said, and she settled back into the action. I was new here. I wasn't about to be the one to tell her that it was all fake.

So I watched with her as Rex Runyon got a second wind and came back at El Gigantico, jumping on his back and bringing him to the mat like David slaying Goliath. The sun slowly set over the water while, downstairs, Norman dragged in the rest of his mannequins neck-first. Mira clapped her hands and cheered, with absolute faith, while Cat Norman sat in the windowsill, licking his paws one by one, as my summer began.

chapter two

We watched wrestling for about an hour. There were four matches, several arguments, and two referees chucked into the action and beaten severely.

"So," Mira said finally, clicking off the TV as the local news came on, "I am dying for a grilled chicken salad. Are you hungry?"

"Yeah," I said, realizing I was.

"Well, there's a place just up on the corner," she told me. "The food is *great*."

"Okay," I said, getting up and digging into my pocket for the money my mother had slipped me as I'd gotten on the train.

"Wait, wait. It's your first night. Let me treat." She picked up her purse—a big pink vinyl thing, which had to be a thrift shop find—drew out her wallet, and selected a twenty, which she held out to me.

"Aren't you coming?" I asked.

"Oh, no, I'll stay here. I've already been to town once today. And this way you can get a feel for the place, find your bearings, right?" she said easily, pulling the pen out of her hair and repositioning it with a jab. "Besides, there's only room on the bike for one, unless you want to ride on the handlebars. But the last time we tried that, I hit a rock and Norman got pitched off and crash-landed into this fence and a bunch of poison ivy. It was just *awful*."

"Wait," I said, struggling to catch up. "The bike?"

"Yep. She's out front." She stood up, tightening the belt on her kimono. "Don't worry, there's a light and everything. And it's a straight shot up to the Last Chance. Just watch out for the huge pothole and the Masons' rottweiler and you're home free."

"What?"

"Their chicken Caesar salad is so *good!*" she said. She was already heading toward the kitchen, the door creaking as she pushed it open. "And you just get whatever you want, okay?"

I turned to say something, but she was already gone, humming under her breath, as if she'd forgotten me already. I looked at the note on the door—BELL—and felt like I'd been caught up in some wild cyclone, like Dorothy thrown into Oz, with not a good witch in sight to save me.

But my stomach was growling, so I looked at the bike, thought better of it, and set off on foot down the steps, past the brightness of the porch light, into the dark.

○

The Last Chance Bar and Grill was a small building on the corner, right before the exit to the bridge that crossed over to the mainland. It had one lone streetlight, a few parking places, and a neon sign that said, Mira style, FOOD.

When I walked in, the first thing I saw was a tall bony girl throwing some kind of a fit.

"I am telling you," she was saying to another girl, a curvy blonde with her hand on her hip. "If I get less than fifteen percent again tonight I am going to *kill* someone."

"Uh-huh," the blonde said. She was standing by the coffee machine, watching it brew.

"Mark my words," said the bony girl. She had a short haircut with bangs straight across her forehead. She turned and looked toward the back corner of the restaurant, where a group of men in suits were standing up and pushing in their chairs, making leaving noises.

The blonde turned from the coffee machine and looked at me. She had on bright red lipstick. "Can I help you?"

"I need to order some takeout," I said. My voice sounded loud in the almost-empty room.

"Menu's right there," she said, pointing to a stack right beside my elbow. She was staring at my lip. "Let me know when you're ready."

The tall girl brushed past me as she came out from behind the counter, then stepped aside as the suits left. One man toward the back was chewing on a toothpick, smacking his lips. The blonde settled in against the opposite side of the counter, watching me.

"Y'all have a good night," the tall girl said.

"You too," one of the men mumbled.

I went back to scanning the menu, all of it standard beach food: fried seafood, burgers, onion rings, the kind of stuff that had been banned from our house since my mother was born again as Kiki Sparks. It had been months since I'd had a french fry, much less a burger, and my mouth was already watering.

"I knew it," the tall girl said from across the room. She was standing by the table the suits had just abandoned, a bunch of change in her hand. "A dollar seventy. On a thirty-dollar tab."

"Well." The blonde was clearly used to hearing this.

"*Goddammit,*" the tall girl said. "Okay, then. That is *it.*"

The blonde looked at me. "You ready?"

"Yeah."

She took her time coming over, pulling out a ticket from the apron tied loosely around her waist. "Go ahead."

"I'm not going to take this anymore," the tall girl said as she started across the room. She had big, flat feet that smacked the floor with each step.

"Grilled chicken salad," I said, remembering Mira's request, "and a cheeseburger with fries. And onion rings."

The blonde nodded, writing this down. "Anything else?"

"No."

The tall girl stopped right next to me and slammed the handful of change down on the counter, one dime bouncing off to hit the floor with a *ping*. "I can't take it anymore," she said dramatically. "I will remain silent no longer."

"You need ketchup with that?" the blonde said to me, ignoring her.

"Uh, yeah," I said.

The tall girl was taking off her apron, balling it up in her hands. "I don't want to have to do it," she said.

"Mayonnaise?" the blonde asked.

"No," I said.

"I *quit!*" the tall girl announced, throwing her apron at the blonde, who reached up and caught it without even looking. "And now, I will go out and give those rude, inconsiderate fascists a *piece* of my mind." She took two strides to the door, kicked it open with a bang, and was gone. The door swung shut, the screen rattling.

The blonde, still holding the apron, walked to the window and stuck my ticket on a spindle. "Order up."

"All right," a guy's voice said, and then I saw Norman Norman poke his head out and grab the ticket. The blue sunglasses were parked on top of his head. "Where's Morgan?" he asked.

"Quit," the blonde said in a bored voice. She'd pulled out a *Vogue* magazine from somewhere and was flipping the pages.

Norman smiled that sleepy smile, then glanced toward the door and saw me. "Hey, Colie," he said. "This for you and Mira?"

"Yeah," I said. The blonde looked at me again.

"Cool," Norman said, and he waved before disappearing back behind the window.

I stood there, waiting for my food; in the kitchen, a radio was playing softly. About ten minutes passed before the door creaked behind me and the tall girl—Morgan—came back in, mumbling under her breath.

"Already gone?" the blonde said in that same flat voice.

"Drove off just as I got out there," Morgan grumbled. As she passed, the blonde gave her the apron, flipping another page of the magazine.

"Too bad," she said.

"This is the last summer I work here," Morgan declared, pulling her apron strings into a perfect bow. "I mean it."

"I know." The blonde turned another page.

"I'm serious." Morgan went over to the soda machine and filled a cup with ice, shaking some into her mouth and crunching it with a determined look. Then she saw me. "You been helped?"

"Yeah," I said.

"She's Mira's niece," said the blonde.

Morgan looked at me with new interest, eyebrows raised. "Really?"

"You remember. Norman told us about her." The blonde put down her magazine and turned her full attention back to me. "Kiki Sparks' kid. Can you imagine."

"I can't," Morgan said, but she smiled. "What's your name?"

"Colie," I said warily. I'd had enough experience with girls in groups to be on my guard.

"What's the deal with that thing in your lip?" the blonde said bluntly. "It's creepy."

"Isabel," Morgan said, elbowing her. "How old are you, Colie?"

"Fifteen," I said.

Morgan came closer to me, tucking her hair behind her ear. On her right hand, she wore a ring with a tiny diamond, just big enough to flash in the light. "How long you down for?"

"Just the summer," I said.

"Order up!" Norman yelled from the kitchen.

"That's great," Morgan said. "You'll be right next door. Maybe we can go to the movies sometime or something."

"Sure," I said, but I kept my voice low. "That would be—"

"Here you go," Isabel, the blonde, said, dropping my food right in front of me. "Ketchup's inside the box. That'll be fifteen-eighteen with tax."

"Right," I said, handing her the twenty. She turned on her heel and went to the register.

"Well, tell Mira I said hi," Morgan said, "and that I'll be by for Triple Threat tomorrow, since I'm off."

"Triple Threat," I repeated. That *had* to have something to do with wrestling. "Okay. I will."

"Here's your change," Isabel said, slapping it on top of one of the boxes.

"Thanks," I said.

She stepped back, next to Morgan, and squinted at me. "Can I tell you something?" she said.

"No," Morgan told her, her voice low.

I didn't say anything. So she did.

"That thing in your lip is, like, repulsive." She scrunched up her nose as she said it.

"Isabel," Morgan said sternly in a Mom voice. "Stop it."

"And next time you decide to dye your hair," Isabel went on, ignoring her, "you should try to get all of it one color. I'm sure your mom can afford to send you to a professional."

"*Isabel,*" Morgan said, grabbing her by the arm. Then she looked at me. "Colie," she said, like she knew me. "Just don't listen . . ."

But I didn't hear her, couldn't, was already gone, turning and walking out the door with the food in my hands to the parking lot before I even knew what was happening. Over the years I had perfected removing myself from situations. It was kind of like automatic pilot; I just shut down and retreated, my brain clicking off before anything that hurt could sink in.

But every once in a while, something would get through. Now I stood under that one streetlight and the fries and onion rings stank in my hands. I wasn't hungry anymore. I wasn't even me anymore. I was bigger, a year younger, and back in my neighborhood the night Chase Mercer and I took that walk down to the eighteenth hole.

I didn't cry as I walked back to Mira's house. You get to a point where you just can't. It never stops hurting. But I was glad when I didn't cry anymore.

I didn't even know this girl, this Isabel with her blonde hair and pouty lips. It was like I wore a permanent "Kick Me" sign, not only at home and school but out in the rest of the world, too. *It isn't fair,* I thought, but those words were as meaningless as all the rest.

Mira was sitting in front of the TV when I came in. She'd put

26

on a pair of blue old-lady slippers and replaced the kimono with a faded plaid bathrobe.

"Colie?" she called out. "Is that you?"

"Yes," I said.

"Did you find it okay?"

I looked at myself in the full-length mirror by the door: my black hair, my piercing, my torn-up jeans and black shirt, long-sleeved even in this summer heat. Isabel had hated me on sight, and not because I was fat. Just because she could.

"Colie?" Mira called out again.

"Yeah," I said. "Your salad's right here." I took it into the back room. She opened the box immediately and popped a piece of lettuce into her mouth.

"Oh, I just love their Caesar dressing!" she said happily. "Norman sneaks some home to me every once in a while. It's wonderful. What did you get?"

"Just a burger and fries. Here's your change." I put it on the coffee table, where she had two plates and two iced teas and a stack of napkins waiting.

"Oh, thank you. Now sit down and let's eat. I'm ravenous." Cat Norman hauled himself out from under the couch and nudged the bottom of the box with his nose.

"I'm not that hungry," I said.

"Bad cat," she said, pushing him back with one foot. To me she added, "But you must be starving! You've had such a long day, all this excitement."

"I'm really tired," I said. "I think I'll just turn in."

"Oh." She stopped eating, glancing up at me. "What's wrong?"

"Nothing." This came instantly, like a reflex.

"You sure?"

I thought of Isabel, the way her eyes narrowed as she zeroed in on me. Of my mother in her purple windsuit, new shoes squeaking, waving good-bye. Of an entire summer stretching ahead. "Yes," I said. "I'm sure."

"Well, okay," she said slowly as if we were striking a bargain. "You probably are worn out."

"Yeah," I said, starting out of the room, my cold smelly burger still in my hand. "I am."

"Okay, well, then good night!" she called after me as I started out of the room. "And if you change your mind . . ."

"Okay," I said, "thanks." But she was already settling back in her chair, Cat Norman leaping with a bit of effort to the arm beside her. She turned up the volume on yet another wrestling match, and I could hear the crowd roar, cheering and screaming, as I climbed the stairs to my room.

"Colie!"

It wasn't morning. The room was dark, with the moon big and yellow and hanging just where I'd left it in the corner of the window.

"Colie!"

I sat up in bed, forgetting for a second where I was. Then it came back: the train, Norman, wrestling, Isabel's beauty tips. My face was dry and tight, my eyelashes sticky from the crying I didn't do anymore.

"Colie?" It was Mira, her voice right outside my door. "You have company, honey."

"Company?"

"Yes. Downstairs." She tapped the door with her fingers before walking away. I wondered if I was dreaming.

I pulled my jeans back on and opened the door, looking down the stairs at the lighted room below. This had to be a joke. I didn't even get company at home, much less at a place I'd been less than a day.

I started down the stairs, squinting as the light got brighter and brighter. Everything felt strange, as if I'd been sleeping forever. I was close to the bottom when I saw a set of feet, in sandals, by the door. Two more steps and there were legs, knees, and a small waist with a windbreaker knotted around it. Another two steps, and the beginnings of blonde hair, a pair of pouty lips, and then those same eyes, narrowed at me. I stopped where I was.

"Hey," Isabel said. She had her arms crossed over her chest. "Got a second?"

I hesitated, thinking of Caroline Dawes and all the girls like her I'd left behind.

"I just want to talk to you, okay?" she snapped, as if I'd already said no. Then she took a deep breath and glanced outside. This seemed to settle her down. "Okay?"

I don't know why, but I said, "Okay."

She turned and went out on the front porch, leaving the screen door in half-swing for me to catch. Then she leaned against one of the posts, bit her lip, and looked out into the yard. Up close, I hated to admit, she was even prettier: a classic heart-

29

shaped face, big blue eyes, and pale skin without a zit in sight. Somehow that made it easier to dislike her.

Neither one of us said anything.

"Look," she said suddenly. "I'm *sorry*, okay?" She said this defensively, as if I'd demanded it of her.

I just looked at her.

"What?" she said. "What else do you want?"

"Isabel." Morgan stepped out of the shadows by the bottom of the steps. Her face was stern. "You know that is not how we discussed it."

"It is too," Isabel snapped.

"Do it like I told you," Morgan said evenly. "Like you mean it."

"I can't—" Isabel said.

"Do it. Now." Morgan came up to the second step and nodded toward me. "Go ahead."

Isabel turned back to face me, smoothing her hair. "Okay," she began, "I am sorry I said what I said. I tend to be very critical of what I don't . . ." Here she paused, looking at Morgan.

"Understand," Morgan prompted.

"Understand," Isabel repeated. "What I said was rude and hurtful and uncalled-for. I'd understand if you never respected me again." She looked at Morgan, eyebrows raised.

"But?" Morgan said, prodding her.

"But," Isabel grumbled, "I hope that you can forgive me."

Morgan smiled, nodding at her. "Thank you." Then she looked at me.

"It's okay," I said, taking the hint. "Don't worry about it."

"Thanks," Isabel said. She was already inching off the porch, toward the steps.

"See?" Morgan said to her, squeezing her arm. "*That* wasn't so hard, now was it?"

"I'm going home," Isabel told her, her duty done. She was lighter on her feet now, practically bounding down the steps and across the yard to the little white house I'd seen earlier.

Morgan sighed. Close up she looked older and pointier: bony elbows, prominent collarbone, a nose that jutted out sharp and sudden.

"She's not so bad," she said to me, as if I'd said otherwise. "She can just be a real bitch sometimes. Mark says she's friend-ship impaired."

"Mark?" I said.

"My fiancé." She smiled and extended her right hand, that tiny diamond twinkling.

There was a sudden burst of music from the little house. Lights were coming on in the windows, and I caught a glimpse of Isabel passing by.

"Then why do you put up with her?" I asked.

She looked over at the house; the music was cheerful, bouncy and wild, and now Isabel was dancing, a beer in one hand. She shimmied past the windows, shaking her hair, hips swaying. Morgan smiled.

"Because, for the most part, she's all I've got," she said. And then she went down the steps, across the yard, and up the path to that little house. When she got to the doorstep she turned and waved.

"See you around," she said.

"Okay," I said.

I watched as she opened the door, the music spilling out; it was disco, some woman wailing. And as Morgan stepped in, Isabel whirled by, grinning, and grabbed her arm, pulling her into that warm light before the door swung shut behind them.

chapter three

The next morning, when I went in to the bathroom to brush my teeth, I noticed the index card over the sink.

RIGHT FAUCET DRIPS EASILY, it said. TIGHTEN WITH WRENCH AFTER USING. And then there was an arrow, pointing down to where a small wrench was tied with bright red yarn to one of the pipes.

This is crazy, I thought.

But that wasn't all. In the shower, HOT WATER IS VERY HOT! USE WITH CARE was posted over the soap dish. And on the toilet: HANDLE LOOSE. DON'T YANK. (As if I had some desire to do *that.*) The overhead fan was clearly BROKEN, the tiles by the door were LOOSE so I had to WALK CAREFULLY. And I was informed, cryptically, that the light over medicine cabinet WORKS, BUT ONLY SOMETIMES.

They were all over the house. I came across them like

dropped bread crumbs, leading me from one thing to another. Windows were PAINTED SHUT, banisters LOOSE, chairs had ONE LEG TOO SHORT. It was like a strange game, and it made me feel unsteady and weird, wishing that even one thing was new enough to work perfectly. I wondered how anyone could live like this, but it was obvious that Mira wasn't just anyone.

Before I got to Colby, all I knew was that she was two years older than my mother, unmarried, and had inherited all of my grandparents' money. I also knew that, like us, she was overweight. Mira had lived in Chicago during the first few years we'd crisscrossed the country in our Volaré, and the one thing I clearly remembered about visiting her were the doughnuts she'd made out of Pillsbury biscuit dough, fried and rolled in cinnamon and sugar. She always seemed to be cooking or eating.

When my mother got thin, it was like she'd found religion. She wanted to share it with everyone: me first, followed by the legions of women who flocked to her aerobics classes, and then the rest of the free world. She was like an evangelist of weight loss. But it was clear Mira hadn't converted: the closet in my room contained every bit of Kiki merchandise ever manufactured, all of it stacked and neat in its original packaging. (I'd added mine to the pile.) And that morning Mira made doughnuts. I sat and watched her eat five of them, *pop pop pop pop pop,* one right after another, licking her fingers and laughing that giggly laugh all the way.

Mira had been my grandparents' favorite: art school educated, full of promise, the good daughter. My mother, on the other hand, with her wild clothes and lifestyle, had fallen entirely out of favor when she'd gotten pregnant at twenty, dropped out of college, and had me. We spent so much time moving around that her family hardly ever knew where we lived, much less who we were. Our few visits to Mira's had ended with big blowouts, usually sparked by some childhood memory she and my mother recalled differently. The last time I'd seen her was at my grandmother's funeral, in Cincinnati, when I was about ten. We'd stuck around just long enough to find out Mira was inheriting everything; not too long after, she'd moved to Colby.

After I ate two doughnuts, I realized those forty-five-and-a-half pounds could creep back easily over a whole summer of what my mother termed "Stuffin' for Nothin'." I ran on the beach for an hour, Walkman on, music pounding in my ears.

When I got back I found Mira in her studio, a big messy room off the kitchen. She wore yellow overalls and her slippers, and her hair was piled up on top of her head, with about seven pens, capped and uncapped, sticking out in various places.

"Do you want to see my new death card?" she asked me cheerfully. "I've been working on it all week."

"Death card?"

"Well, technically it's called a condolence card," she said, shifting in her office chair, which was jacked up as high as it could go. "But it is what it is, you know?"

I took the two pieces of thick sketch paper she handed me. On the first was a pastel drawing of some flowers, over which was written:

I am so sorry . . .

And on the second, which was to be the inside of the card:

All losses are so hard to bear, but the loss of former love can be the hardest. Regardless of the reasons, there was love. And my heart and thoughts are with you at this difficult time.

"Too much?" she said as I looked down at the bottom of the page, where *Mira's Miracles* was written in small print, with tiny red hearts topping both *i*'s.

"Um, no," I said. "I just never saw a card that specific before."

"It's the new wave," she said simply, pulling a pen out of her hair. "Specialized condolence cards for new occasions. Dead ex-husbands, dead bosses, dead mailmen . . ."

I looked at her.

"I'm serious!" she said, spinning around in her chair and reaching for a box behind her. "Here it is!" She produced a card and cleared her throat. "The outside says, *I considered him a friend. . . .* And when you open it up, it reads, *Sometimes a service can become more than just routine, when it is delivered with heart and humor and personal care. I considered him to be my friend and I will miss so much our daily contact.*" She looked at me, grinning. "See what I mean?"

"You give that to your mailman?" I said.

"To your mailman's *widow*," she corrected me, chucking the card back into the box. "I have them for everything, every profession. You have to. People's lives are very specialized now. Their cards need to be, too."

"I don't know if I'd buy a card for my mailman's widow."

"You might not," she said seriously. "But you are probably not a card person. Some people just *need* to give cards. And they're the ones that keep me in business."

I looked at the shelves against the back wall, all of them stacked with boxes and boxes of cards. "Did you do all of these?"

"Yep. I've done about two or three a week since art school." She gestured towards them. "I mean, I have cards here from ten, fifteen years back."

"Do you only do death cards?" I asked her.

"Well, I started out with the standard line," she said, straightening a can of pens on her desk. "Birthdays, valentines, et cetera. But then I hit big in the eighties with NonniCards."

"Wait," I said suddenly. "I know that name."

She smiled, reaching under her desk and coming up with another card. "Yep, she was the motherlode. Nonni made me my name in this business."

I immediately recognized the little girl in a sailor suit and her mother's high-heeled shoes. She'd been a greeting card star, the next big wave after Garfield the cat. I could remember begging my mother for a Nonni doll at a gas station once when I knew we couldn't afford it.

"Oh my God," I said, looking up at Mira. "I never knew she was yours."

"Yep," she said, smiling fondly at the card. "She had her run. Then, after all the hype, I was really in the mood to focus on something different. And condolences just interested me. They'd hardly been explored."

I was staring all the time at all those boxes, shelves upon shelves. A lifetime of death. "Do you ever run out of ideas?"

"Not really," she said, her slippered feet, blue and fuzzy, dangling above the floor. "You'd be *amazed* how many ways there are to say you're sorry in the world. I haven't even begun to discover them all."

"Still," I said. "That's a lot of dead mailmen."

She looked surprised, her eyes wide. Then she laughed, one single burst of "Ha!" A pen fell out of her hair, clattering to the floor. She ignored it. "I guess you're right," she said, looking up at the shelves again. "It sure is."

Cat Norman dragged himself up on the windowsill, settling his girth along its narrow width. Outside, Mira's collection of birdfeeders was swinging in the wind, several birds perched on each. Cat Norman lifted one paw and tapped the glass. Then he yawned and closed his eyes in the sun.

"So," Mira said to me. "It's your first day. You should go exploring, check out the town or something."

"Maybe I will," I said, just as the front door slammed.

"It's me," someone called out.

"Norman Norman," Mira called back. "We're in here."

Norman poked his head in, looked around, and stepped inside. He was barefoot, in jeans and a green T-shirt with a pair of red, square-framed sunglasses hooked over the collar. His hair, just to his shoulders, wasn't long enough to be truly hippie-annoying, but it was close.

"So, Norman," Mira said, uncapping another pen and outlining a tree on a new piece of paper, "any decent finds this morning?"

He grinned. "Oh, man. It was a *good* day. I got four more ash-trays for that sculpture—one's a souvenir from Niagara Falls—and an old blender, plus a whole boxful of bicycle gears."

I *knew* it, I thought. Art freak.

"Wow," Mira said, pulling a pen out of her hair. "No sunglasses?"

"Three pairs," Norman said. "One with purple lenses."

"It *was* a good day," she said. To me she added, "Norman and I are *into* yard sales. I've furnished practically this whole house with secondhand stuff."

"Really," I said, eyeing the cracked fishtank.

"Oh, sure," she said, not noticing. "You'd be amazed at what some people will throw away! Now, if I just had time to fix everything, I'd be all set."

Norman picked up a sketch, glanced at it, then put it back down on the table. "I saw Bea Williamson this morning," he said in a low voice. "Lurking about looking for cut glass."

"Oh, of course," Mira said with a sigh. "Did she have it with her?"

Norman nodded solemnly. "Yep. I swear, I think it's almost gotten . . . bigger."

Mira shook her head. "Not possible."

"I'm serious," Norman said. "It's *way* big."

I kept waiting for someone to expand on this, but since neither of them seemed about to, I asked, "What are you talking about?"

They looked at each other. Then, Mira took a breath. "Bea Williamson's baby," she said quietly, as if someone could hear us, "has the biggest head you have ever seen."

Norman nodded, seconding this.

"A baby?" I said.

"A big-headed baby," Mira corrected me. "You should see the cranium on this kid. It's mind-boggling."

"She's going to be *very* bright," Norman said.

"Well, she *is* a Williamson." Mira sighed, as if that explained everything. Then, to me, she added, "They're very important in Colby, the Williamsons."

"Mean," Norman explained.

Mira shook her head, waving him off with one hand. "Now, now," she said. "So, Norman. I was just telling Colie she should go exploring today. You know, she met Isabel and Morgan last night."

"Yeah," Norman said, smiling at me in a way that made me look over at the birdfeeders, quick. "I heard."

"Very nice girls," Mira pronounced. "Although Isabel, like Bea Williamson, can be somewhat of a pill. But she's good at heart."

"Yeah." Norman scuffed his bare foot against the floor. "She's got nothing on Bea Williamson."

"*Everyone* is good at heart," Mira said simply, fixing me with a look that made me feel strange. "It's true," she added, as if she thought I wouldn't quite believe her, and I looked into her bright eyes and wondered what she meant.

"I'm going to the library," Norman said. "You got anything that needs to be returned?"

"Oh, Norman, you are my saint," Mira said cheerfully, swiveling to point to a stack of books by the far window. To me she added, "Without him I would flail about, lost and bewildered."

"That's not true," Norman said.

"Oh, Norman," Mira said with a sigh. "I don't know what I'll do when you leave me." Then she added, "It's a long bike ride to the library. *Lots* of potholes."

"It's no problem," Norman said. "So, Colie. You want to come?"

Mira was already back at work, humming softly under her breath. Under the drafting table she had one leg crossed over the other, one blue slipper bouncing up and down, up and down.

"I guess," I said. "I mean, I need to change."

"Take your time," he told me, picking up the books and starting that slow amble toward the door. "I'll be outside."

I went upstairs and washed my face, then pulled my hair back in a ponytail and put on a different shirt. From my window I could see Norman; he was wearing the red sunglasses and stretched out across the hood of the car, his feet hanging off the edge. He was kind of cute, if you liked that Deadhead type. Which I didn't.

I looked at myself in the mirror; with my hair up I looked twelve. I took it down. Put it up again. Then changed my shirt and checked on Norman, who appeared to have fallen asleep, baking in the sun.

I changed my shirt again, put on my Walkman and went downstairs.

"Ready?" he said as soon as I stepped outside, startling me. He hadn't been sleeping, after all.

"Sure," I said, and got in. The seat was hot on the back of my legs. Norman opened the glove compartment, and about six pairs of sunglasses fell out, all different kinds: Ray•Bans, purple-framed old-lady glasses, wraparound seventies styles.

"Oops," he said, reaching over and collecting them. "Sorry." He traded the pair he'd been wearing for some green ones and put them on, shoving the rest back into the glove compartment, which he slammed shut. It immediately fell open.

"Damn," he said, pushing it shut again.

"Are all those yours?" I asked, as it opened and another pair fell out.

"Yeah," he said, finally closing it with a good whack. "I collect them." He started up the car. "You need a pair?"

"No," I said.

"Okay," he said simply, shrugging. "Whatever."

We backed out of the driveway.

"Whatcha listening to?" he asked, pointing to the head-phones around my neck.

"Fierces of Fuquay," I said.

"Who?"

"Fierces of Fuquay," I repeated.

"Never heard of them," he announced. Now he pointed to the tape deck. "Pop it in."

So I did. It wasn't really fair, because it came on in the middle of this song called "Bite," where the lead singer was just screaming over the drums. Norman's face looked pained, as if someone was stepping on his foot.

When the song ended, he said, "You like that?"

"Yes," I said, popping it out and back into my Walkman.

"Why?"

"Why?" I repeated.

"Yeah."

"Because I just do," I said.

"Shit," he said loudly, and I was about to tell him I thought the same thing of whatever hippie music *he* listened to when I realized he was staring, mouth open, across the street at the Last Chance Bar and Grill. Two big buses, each with *Family Beach Getaways* painted on the sides, were pulling into the tiny parking lot.

"What is it?" I said.

"Gotta take a detour," he told me. He hit the gas and we lurched forward, pulling up just as the bus door wheezed open and people started filing off, all in visors and bathing suits with children clinging to various parts of them. Norman got out of the wagon and went around to the back, letting down the tailgate to pull out a pair of shoes. He started toward the front entrance, dodging the bus passengers.

"Come on," he said, dropping the shoes on the ground and stepping into them. "We might need you."

I followed him up the steps, where a line was already forming; bodies shifting, voices irritated. Norman pushed through, yelling, "Excuse me! We work here!" and people let him pass, with me trying to keep up behind him.

The first thing I saw was a stunned Morgan standing behind the counter watching the line form.

"Help us!" she yelled at Norman, who waved her off and went back into the kitchen. Through the food window I could see another cook, an older man with bushy red hair.

Isabel walked up, carrying a stack of menus. "There are at least seventy total," she said to Morgan.

"Seventy?" Morgan shrieked. "Are they kidding?"

"We can seat fifty-five," Isabel told her. "The rest can stand or wait. That's it."

"This is insane," Morgan said, watching as the tables quickly filled up. Isabel was already darting from one to another, handing out menus and silverware. "I can't *do* this."

"How many we got?" Norman yelled through the food window.

"Seventy," Morgan told him. "There's no way, it's too many and we only have two cooks and this place is too—"

"Don't break down on me," Isabel said as she pushed her way behind the counter. "I need you now, Morgan, okay?"

"I can't—" Morgan replied, wringing her hands.

"Yes, you can," Isabel said calmly. "Now you take half and I'll take half. There's no other way."

"Oh, my God," Morgan moaned, tightening her apron.

"Do it," Isabel said. She glanced toward the line, her lips moving as she counted those still standing. Then she saw me.

"You," she said, pointing. Everyone in line looked at each other, then at me. "Yeah, you. Lip girl."

So much for apologies. "What?" I said.

"Want to make yourself useful?"

I thought about it. I knew I didn't owe her anything. But then again, I had a whole summer stretching ahead of me.

"Good," she said, deciding for me before I even opened my mouth. And as I came closer she picked up the shovel for the ice, slapped it in my hand, and pointed to the soda machine. "Get to work."

chapter four

I never set out to be a waitress. But just like that, I had a job.

It was Morgan's idea, of course.

"We do need some extra help," she said to Isabel, who was sitting at the end of the counter after that frantic lunch, arranging her money. Morgan was upending ketchup bottles, one on top of another, mixing and marrying their contents. "Ever since Hillary ran off with that Cuban guy we've been shorthanded. Bick and Norman can handle things back in the kitchen. But since Ron's in Barbados all summer, he's not around to run things, which leaves more for me and you to do."

"We're fine," Isabel said

"Oh, yeah," Morgan said, facing her. She had a smear of ketchup across one cheek. "You would have been just fine with out Colie getting you all those sodas *and* answering the phone."

"You have ketchup on your face," Isabel told her

Morgan wiped her hand across both cheeks. "Gone?" she said.

"Yep." Isabel stood and stretched her arms over her head, her ample bosom rising and falling as she did so.

"So?" Morgan said. "Come on, Isabel. Another day like today with no backup and we'd be screwed. You know it."

Isabel picked up the stack of bills from the counter, folded it, and slid it in her back pocket. Then she looked at me. "We can't pay much," she said. "Just minimum, plus tips. That's it."

"It'll be fun, Colie," Morgan said. "You should do it."

"Waitressing sucks," Isabel told me. "A lot of people can't handle it."

"Oh, it's not so awful." Morgan shook a ketchup bottle, knocking out the dregs. "Besides, we have a good time, right?"

"I mean, it's up to you," Isabel said, walking toward the door. "I, myself, would think long and hard about it."

"Just say yes." Morgan whispered to me as Isabel pushed open the door, putting on a pair of red-framed sunglasses.

"Yes," I said. "I'll take it."

"Fine," Isabel said. "You start tomorrow morning. Be here at nine-thirty." The door slammed behind her, and I could hear gravel crunching as she walked across the parking lot to a beat-up black VW Rabbit parked crookedly across two spaces. She opened the door and climbed in, reaching up to pull a key from under the visor. The radio was already blasting as she sped out in reverse, spraying gravel everywhere.

"Congratulations," Morgan said, handing me a bottle of ketchup. "Welcome to the Last Chance."

O

Later that afternoon when I was standing across the street from the restaurant, waiting for the traffic light to change, I saw something in the distance. It began as a speck, hardly visible, and then grew larger and larger as it approached, until I could make out a color—red—and a noise, too. A bell.

By the time I recognized Mira's crazy red bike, there was a group of customers coming out of the Last Chance. They were college girls, all in sunglasses and T-shirts with damp spots where their bathing suits had soaked through. *Day-trippers,* Isabel had said snidely, like it was a slur of some kind. They were talking, heading back to the beach, when they heard it, too.

Ching-ching! It was high-pitched, one of those old-timey bells like paperboys used in the movies, and as the bike got closer it got louder. The girls stopped talking and we all watched as Mira came into view.

She was still wearing her yellow overalls, rolled up at the cuff, and a worn pair of purple high-tops. Her hair was flowing out behind her, long and red and wild, like some kind of living cape. And, finally, she was wearing sunglasses: black wraparound frames, like the Terminator. All of the reflectors on her battered bike glinted as she came closer.

And she kept ringing that bell. *Ching-ching! Ching-ching!*

"Oh, my God," one of the daytripper girls said, laughing. "What the hell is *that?*"

Mira was nearing the intersection. The girls started to move toward their car, still giggling and watching, but she didn't notice them. She only saw me.

"Colie!" she called, waving one hand wildly, as if there was any way I could have missed her. "Over here!"

I could feel the girls looking at me, and my face began to burn. I lifted one hand, just barely, and wished the parking lot would open up and suck me in.

"I'm going to the market to buy some more biscuit dough!" she screamed as a big truck rumbled by. "You want anything?!"

I managed to shake my head.

"Okay!" she yelled, flashing me a thumbs-up. "I'll see you later, then!" And with that, she started out into traffic, pedaling slowly at first, dodging the occasional pothole, and then coasting down the hill toward the rest of town.

As Mira passed, the road began to dip and she started picking up speed, the wheel spokes blurring. People in cars were watching her, the day-tripper girls, tourists at the gas station, everyone, even me. We all stared as her hair began to stream behind her again, a reflector on the back of the bike catching the sunlight and sparkling before she took the next curve and disappeared.

"Mayonnaise," Morgan said, "is a lot like men."

It was nine-thirty in the morning on my first day of work, but I'd been up since six. I kept thinking Morgan would forget me or change her mind but at nine-fifteen she pulled up in front of Mira's steps and beeped her horn, just as we'd planned.

The restaurant was empty except for us and the radio, tuned to an oldies station. "Twisting the Night Away" was playing, and we were making salad dressing, both of us up to our elbows in thick, smelly mayonnaise.

"It can," she went on, plopping another scoop into the bowl, "make everything much better, adding flavor and ease to your life. Or, it can just be sticky and gross and make you nauseous."

I smiled, stirring my mayonnaise while I considered this. "I hate mayonnaise."

"You'll probably hate men too, from time to time," she said. "At least mayonnaise you can avoid."

This was the way Morgan taught. Not in instructions, but pronouncements. Everything was a lesson.

"Lettuce," she announced later, pulling a head out of the plastic bag in front of us, "should be leafy, not slimy. And no black or brown edges. We use lettuce on everything: garnish, salads, burgers. A bad piece of lettuce can ruin your whole day."

"Right," I said.

"Chop it like this," she instructed, taking a few whacks with a knife before handing it to me. "Big chops, but not too big."

I chopped. She watched. "Good," she said, reaching over to adjust my chops just a bit. I went on. "Very good."

Morgan was this meticulous about everything. Preparing dressings was a ritual, every measurement carefully checked. Isabel, on the other hand, dumped it all in at once, knocked a spoon around, and came up with the same results, dipping in a finger and licking it to double-check.

But Morgan had her own way.

"Peel carrots away from you," she said, demonstrating, "and cut off the ends about a quarter inch each. When feeding them into the processor, pause about every five seconds. It gives a finer shred."

I peeled, chopped, and stocked. I learned the perfect, sym-

49

metrical way to stack coffee cups and sugar packets, to fold rags at a right angle against flat surfaces, clean side up. Morgan kept the counter area spick-and-span, each element in its place. When she was nervous, she went around correcting things.

"Take-out boxes on the *left,* cup lids on the *right,*" she'd shout, slamming them around as she restored order to her uni verse. "And spoons are handle side *up,* Isabel."

"Yeah, yeah," Isabel would say. When she was mad or just bored she purposely rearranged things just to see how long it took Morgan to find them. It was like a passive-aggressive trea-sure hunt.

That first lunch, when Norman and I had stopped to pitch in, was a constant blur of people and noise and food. Everyone was screaming at each other, Isabel and Morgan running past with orders, Norman flipping burgers and yelling things to Bick, the other cook, who stayed stonily quiet and cool the en-tire time. I shoveled ice like my life depended on it, answered the phone and took orders although I knew almost nothing about the menu, and messed up the register so badly it stuck on $10,000.00 and beeped for fifteen minutes straight before Isabel, in a fit of rage, whacked it with a plastic water pitcher. It was Us against Them, clearly, and for once I was part of Us. I didn't really know what I was doing; I had to go on faith. So I just handed out my drinks and grabbed the phone when it screamed, wrapping the cord around my wrist and stabbing the pen Mor-gan had tossed me in my hair, the same way Isabel wore hers, and fought on.

"Last Chance," I'd shout over the din. "Can I help you?"

And now, I was doing it every day.

At first, just walking up to a table full of strangers had scared me to death. I couldn't even make eye contact, stuttering through the basic questions Morgan had taught me—*What would you like to drink? Have you decided? How would you like that cooked? Fries or hush puppies?*—my hand literally shaking as it moved across my order pad. It made me nervous to stand there so exposed, all of those people *looking* at me.

But then, on about my third table, I finally got the nerve to glance up and realized that, basically, they *weren't*. For the most part, they were flipping through the menu, extracting Sweet'n Low packets from their toddler's grip, or so lost in their own conversation that I didn't even register: twenty minutes later they'd be flagging Isabel down, sure *she* was the one with their check. They didn't know or care about me. To them, I was just a waitress, a girl with an apron and a tea pitcher; they didn't even seem to notice my lip ring. And that was fine with me.

"In this job," Morgan told me after a dinner rush, "You get a lifetime of experience every day. A crisis will crop up, worsen, come to a head and resolve itself all in fifteen to thirty minutes. You don't even have time to panic. You just push through."

She was right. For every burger overcooked, salad with the wrong dressing, or missing order of fries, there was a solution. Each time I got a little faster, a little stronger, a little bit more confident. Even Isabel was my ally.

"He's an asshole," she said over her shoulder after a grumpy tourist had snapped at me for giving him unsweetened tea instead of sweetened. "He's on vacation, for God's sake. He should lighten up!"

Finally, no matter how bad it got, or how rude anyone was,

they were gone within an hour, tops. After what I was used to, this was nothing.

My mother, however, expressed concern. "Honey," she said, her voice crackling through all those phone lines stretched across the ocean, "you should be having fun. You don't need to work."

"Mom, I like it," I said, admitting to her what I was careful to remain blasé about at the restaurant: that I actually enjoyed it. I felt like I was holding my breath, fingers crossed, as if at any moment it could be over, just like that.

I assured my mother that I was not stuffing myself with onion rings and was running every day, which made her feel a little better. And I didn't bring up Mira's signs, or her bike, or her collection of broken furniture. My mother was prone to overreactions.

She was distracted, anyway, about to embark on a tour of Italy which included a huge, open-air aerobics session on a soccer field. Hundreds of women would be step-kicking and lunging along with her, and my little waitressing job would be soon forgotten.

But not by me. Because I had a friend.

"Colie," Morgan said at the end of that first week, after we'd locked the door behind the last customer and mopped the floor. My feet hurt and I smelled like grease, but that night I'd made fifty bucks, all mine. "Come on. I want to show you something."

I followed her out the back door and up some steps to the roof, which was flat and sticky and smelled like tar. All around us it was dark, with places lit up here and there: I could see the supermarket and the bridge, as well as one lone circling searchlight from the car dealership.

"Can you see that?" she said. "Right there." She pointed over the trees to a bright spot nearby, close enough to make out if I stood at the very edge of the roof.

"It's Maverick Stadium," she said. "That's where Mark used to play." Mark, Morgan's fiancé, was someone I already felt I knew. She talked about him constantly. How he wore boxers, not briefs. How he wanted three kids, two girls and a boy. How his batting average was improving and he'd had two home runs already this season even with a wrist injury. And how he'd asked Morgan to marry him three months ago, on his last night in Colby, as they sat together at the International House of Pancakes saying good-bye.

"I miss him so much," she said. She kept a picture of him— he was literally tall, dark, and handsome—in her wallet. "Only three months left in the season."

"How'd you meet him?" I asked her.

She smiled. "Here, actually. During a dinner rush. He was sitting at the counter and Isabel knocked a cup of coffee in his lap."

"Ouch," I said.

"No kidding. She was so slammed she just kept moving, so I cleaned it up and made all the apologies. He said it was okay, no problem, and I laughed and said pretty girls get away with anything." She looked down, twisting her ring a bit so the diamond sat in the center of her finger. "And he smiled, and looked at Isabel, and said she wasn't his type."

There was a faint cheer from the stadium, and I saw a ball whiz over the far fence and out of sight.

"And so," she went on, "I said, 'Oh really? What is your type, exactly?' and he looked up at me and said, 'You.'" She grinned.

"I mean, Colie, I've spent so long watching guys I liked go after Isabel. When we were in tenth grade, I spent a whole year in love with this guy named Chris Catlock. And then one night he finally called me. I almost *died*. But then . . ."

There was a another cheer from the stadium, followed by an announcer's voice crackling.

". . . he asked me if I could find out if Isabel liked him," she said, wrinkling her nose. "It was awful. I cried for days. But that's what's so amazing about Mark, you know? He picked *me*. He *loves* me." She smiled again, tilting her head back.

I looked at her profile. "You're lucky," I told her.

"Oh, you'll find someone," she said, patting my knee. "You're just a baby still, anyway."

I nodded, my eyes on the distant stadium.

"I know," I said, and I had that feeling again, that all of this could slip away at any moment. I could have been anyone to her.

We stayed on the roof for a long time, Morgan and I. We let our feet dangle over the edge and chewed gum and listened to the game, waiting for the crack of the bat and then whistling and cheering, as the runners dashed toward home.

I worked alternate lunches and dinners at the Last Chance, perfecting my blue cheese dressing and mastering the Cuisinart. But I still had a lot to learn.

"Waiting tables," Morgan said to me one day, "is a lot like life. It's all about attitude."

"Attitude," I repeated, nodding.

"Yours," she went on, gesturing at the restaurant, "and theirs. It's an even equation."

From behind the counter, where she was reading *Vogue,* Isabel made her *hrrumph* noise. Then she turned a page, loudly.

"Some people can do this job," Morgan said. "And some people can't. And it can really suck. Also, as you know by now, you have to be able to handle people being mean to you." She tilted her head to the side, watching me. This was a test.

"I can do that," I said solidly. It was the one thing I was sure of.

Morgan was always close behind me, keeping up a constant chatter of corrections, managing to handle her own section and double-check mine as well.

"Refill that tea at Table Seven," she'd say over her shoulder as she passed, her hands full of dirty plates. "And Six is looking kind of antsy for a check."

"Right," I'd say, and do as she said. Isabel pretty much ignored me, pushing me out of the way to get to the ice machine or pick up her food.

"The important thing to remember," Morgan always said, "is that you are a human being and worthy of respect. Sometimes, customers will make you doubt that."

This I had already learned when a large woman with a run in her pantyhose had asked me the difference between Nachos and Deluxe Nachos.

"Let me check the menu real quick," I said, pulling one out from under my arm. "I'm new and I don't quite—"

"Duh," she said loudly to her friend, rolling her eyes. Her friend, also large, giggled and smacked her gum.

"You are *kidding* me," Morgan said when I told her. We were huddled back by the soda machine. She turned around and eyeballed the table, hand on her hip. "How rude can you be?"

"Obviously pretty rude," Norman said from the other side of the food window, where he was flipping burgers.

"It doesn't matter," I said.

"Of course it does." Morgan turned back around, fixing her pointy gaze right on me. "You are *not stupid,* Colie. Don't let anyone make you think you are. Okay?"

"Okay," I said.

She took a deep breath and rattled it off: "Regular Nachos: beans, chips, cheese, chiles. Deluxe Nachos: all the above plus chicken or beef, tomato, and olives."

"Duh," Norman said loudly.

"Duh indeed," Morgan replied, grabbing a tea pitcher from behind me. "Get back out there," she said to me, nodding toward my section. "There's work to do."

And the pronouncements continued.

"Good attitude, good money," Morgan always said. "Shit attitude, shit money."

"Oh, shut *up* with that already," Isabel would groan, stabbing her pen back in her hair. I don't know what bothered her more, Morgan's advice or that she was sharing it with me.

Despite all of this, Morgan was always the one to crack under the pressure of a busy rush. In my first two weeks, I saw her quit twice. Three times, if you counted my first day in Colby. It was always the same, beginning with some offense in the later part of the night. She'd declare herself fed up, take off her apron and toss it down indignantly, announcing that she was quitting. Then she'd slam out the door to give someone a piece of her mind. But they had always just left, so she'd come back in, grumbling, and tie her apron on again.

Isabel didn't even flinch during these episodes. She never seemed to get ruffled or upset; she took nothing personally. It was clear that Morgan was dramatic enough for both of them.

Some days I pulled double shifts, working for Morgan so she could wait for Mark to call. She was always incredibly grateful. Sometimes I worked for Isabel so she could sleep off a hangover or go to the beach. She wasn't. The most I'd gotten was a bland "Thanks" tossed over her shoulder as she was coming or going. When we worked together she turned the radio up loud, so we didn't have to talk. And after we locked up she usually drove away toward town, leaving me to walk home alone in the dark.

It didn't really bother me. I'd spent years hearing whispers, taunts called across gyms and locker rooms, and I was thankful even for those compared to the insults right to my face. I'd been called *fat* and *easy, slut* and *whore, Hole in One*. So I didn't mind being ignored. For so long, it had been all I wanted.

When I worked lunches I came home in the late afternoon, while Mira was taking her nap. She had to have one every day, just like a toddler; she said she was no good otherwise. I'd take off my shoes and creep around, exploring, all the while careful to listen for the creak of her bedroom door.

Mira wasn't much of a housekeeper. Everything was dusty and there were cobwebs hanging from the corners of the ceiling. The first week I'd taken the initiative with my own room, washing the windows and cleaning under the bed, kicking up an entire colony of dust bunnies and some lost socks. In the downstairs closet I found three vacuum cleaners, all of which were, of course, BROKEN, leaving me to do the best I could with a broom while I wondered, again, about Mira.

She rode her bike everywhere, even at night, when she attached an incredibly bright light to the handlebars, which occasionally blinded oncoming traffic. She lived off grilled chicken salad, homemade doughnuts, and junk cereal. She was constantly beginning projects: among other things, the living room contained a cane chair with a broken seat, halfway re-strung; a china pig with three legs, sitting next to a tube of Super Glue; and a toy bus with two missing wheels and a dented front fender, as if it had been in some kind of very small, violent accident.

I wasn't even going to *ask* about that.

At night, while she sat in front of the TV—JIGGLE TO GET 11—Mira worked on her projects. Nothing ever seemed to get *completely* fixed, just tinkered with and then labeled with a note. I came back one day to find she'd taken apart the alarm clock in my room—which, although I reset it each day, had been CONSISTENTLY FIVE MINUTES BEHIND—and then put it back together. She was very proud of herself until she discovered she'd left out one huge spring. Now, instead of ringing, it made this awful *moaning* sound. The next day I'd snuck out to the drugstore and purchased a nice, new digital clock, which I kept hidden under my bed as if it was contraband and illegal just because it worked.

The strange thing was that she had enough money to buy all new appliances, if she wanted; I'd discovered a stack of bank statements in a lower cabinet while searching for a vegetable steamer.

The evening I found the vacuum cleaners, I came downstairs to find her sitting on the back porch watching TV.

"Mira," I said, after shoving the broom into the closet, "why don't any of these vacuums work?"

She hadn't heard me, her eyes fixed on the TV. I walked down the dark hallway to stand behind her chair. Then I heard my mother's voice.

"My name is Kiki Sparks," she was saying, right there in her trademark windsuit, blonde hair cut and curled, hands on hips in the can-do pose. She was in a fake living room set, with a plant and sofa behind her. "And if you are overweight and have given up, I want you to listen to me. You don't have to be afraid anymore. Because I can help you."

The music started, that same tune I knew so well; I'd seen this infomercial a million times. It was the one that had made my mother a star.

"Mira?" I said softly.

"It's just amazing what she's done," she said suddenly, as we both watched my mother clap her hands and walk toward the studio audience, grabbing a woman to demonstrate how to do a deep knee squat (perfect for toning those glutes!). "You know, I never doubted your mother could get thin. Or conquer the world, for that matter."

I smiled. "I don't think she ever did either."

"She was always so sure of herself." Mira turned around in her chair to look at me, the light of the TV on her face. "Even during those terrible years when you two were moving from place to place, she was never scared. And she'd never take a cent from our parents; just because she was too principled. She wanted to prove to everyone that she could do it. That was always very important to her."

I thought back to the nights we'd slept in the car; to ketchup soup. To the times she'd thought I was sleeping and cried silently, her hands over her face. My mother was strong, to be sure. But nobody was perfect.

Onscreen, my mother was leading the crowd in a touch-step, touch-step, her arms waving over her head. She had a big, bright smile, her muscles flexing and unflexing with each lunge. "Let's go!" she said to them, to us. "I know you can do it! I know you can!"

Mira was watching, leaning in close. "I just love this program. The weight stuff—" she paused, shaking her head. "That's not important to me; we've always been different that way. But I just love to see what she can *do*. It's infectious, you know? That's why I always watch," she said softly, there in the dark, the light from the TV flickering across both of us. "I always watch."

"Me too," I said, and I sat on the floor by her feet. I pulled my legs in against my chest and we watched together as my mother spread the gospel, one touch-step, touch-step at a time.

chapter five

The Colby post office was a tiny little house, one room lined with mailboxes, staffed by an old man who always looked half asleep. After I worked lunches I'd leave from the back door of the restaurant, walk across an empty field, then past an auto shop and a drugstore to come out right by its front door.

There's a kind of radar that you get, after years of being talked about and made fun of by other people. You can almost smell it when it's about to happen, can recognize instantly the sound of a hushed voice, lowered just enough to make whatever is said okay. I had only been in Colby for a few weeks. But I had not forgotten.

I was in the post office picking through the mail one day— bills, a check from Mira's card company, and a postcard from my mother featuring the Venus de Milo in workout wear—when I heard it.

"Well, you know what they say about her." It was a woman's voice, middle-aged and twangy. She was around the corner, behind the next row of mailboxes.

"I've been told some things," a second woman said. You could tell she wanted her friend to go on. She just wasn't ready to contribute yet.

This was also part of what I knew.

"It's no secret," said the first woman. I could hear her shuffling her mail. "I mean, everyone is aware of it."

I stepped back and leaned against the mailboxes, touching my tongue to my piercing. My face was already hot, that uncontrollable red flush that climbed across my skin, rampant, that one dry spot in the back of my throat that no amount of swallowing helped. I might as well have been back at school, standing in the girls' locker room listening to Caroline Dawes announce to her friends that I'd told Chase Mercer my mother would pay him to be my boyfriend.

And that was a *good* day. Now here, months later in a town where I hardly knew anyone, it was happening again.

"She's been like this ever since she moved here," the first woman said. "But it goes beyond just personality quirks, you know? With that bike, and the clothes she wears. Not to mention all the strays she takes in. It's like she's running some kind of weird commune down at the end of that road. It's embarrassing for *all* of us."

"You'd think," her friend said, "that someone would have told her how ridiculous she looks by now."

"Don't you think I've tried?" the first woman said with a sigh. "But it's no use. She's crazy. It's that simple."

I took a deep breath. They weren't talking about me; of course they weren't. They were talking about *Mira*. I thought of her on her bike, pedaling furiously, and my face began to burn again

"Big Norm Carswell's just beside himself that his son is living beneath her house. God *knows* what goes on over there. I don't even want to think about it."

"Is he the football player? Or the basketball star who went to State on that scholarship?"

"Neither," the first woman said. "He's the youngest, Norm's namesake. They never knew what to do with him; the boy didn't play *anything*. He has long hair and I think he's into drugs."

"Oh, that one. He's actually very nice. He came to my yard sale just last week and bought up all my old sunglasses. Said he collects them."

"He has *many* problems," said the first woman. "But then, so does Mira Sparks. I just know she'll end up living out her days alone, getting crazier and crazier, and fatter and fatter—" and her friend snorted once, an oh-you're-terrible laugh—"in that big old drafty house."

"Oh, my," her friend said, savoring this. "That's so sad."

"Well, it's her choice."

I already hated this woman, the way I had learned to hate anyone who talked trash behind someone's back. I was used to the flat-out mean, straight-to-your-face insult, no messing around or mixing of messages. Somehow, there was more dignity in that.

I turned back to the mailboxes, still feeling sorry for Mira, and tucked our mail in my back pocket. Then I heard something behind me. When I turned around, I saw the Big-Headed Baby for the first time.

I recognized her instantly: there was no way not to. She was about two years old, wearing a frilly pink dress and white sandals. Her hair was blond and wispy, and there was a pink elastic ribbon with a bow stretched across her head, which just made it look bigger, if that was possible. She had true-blue eyes and looked up at me, open-mouthed, clutching her skirt in her hand.

Man, I thought. Mira had been right: it was *quite* a cranium, somewhat egg-shaped, the skin on her scalp pale and almost translucent. The rest of her body seemed toylike in comparison.

She stood there and stared at me, the way kids will when they haven't learned it's rude yet. Then she lifted one hand, touching a chubby finger to her lips in the exact place where my piercing was. She held it there, still watching intently, for a few seconds. I couldn't take my eyes off her.

And then, just as quickly as she'd appeared, she turned and toddled back around the corner, her tiny footsteps barely audible on the tile floor.

I was still standing there when the women walked past—the baby clinging to the hand of the taller one—and out the door, the bell clanking behind them. They were talking about someone else now, about husbands and divorces and real estate. They didn't see me.

I watched them go, two middle-aged women in shorts and sandals. The one with the baby had curled blond hair and was

wearing a sweater patterned with sailboats. They stopped outside, still talking, and smiled and waved at a little old woman
with a walker coming up the steps. The baby ran down the front
walk, arms outstretched, toward the white picket fence and the
roses growing across it.

It didn't matter how old you were. There were Caroline
Daweses everywhere.

I stood at the window of the post office, watching them get
into their cars and drive away. Then I walked back to Mira's.

"So," she said with a smile, flipping through the mail. "What's
the word on the street?"

I heard that woman's voice in my head, so snide, and felt that
same dry spot in my throat, the same flush across my skin.

"Nothing," I said.

And she nodded, believing me, before turning back to the
TV.

It was so much easier with wrestling. There was a balance:
you had your good guys, like Rex Runyon, and your bad guys,
like the Bruiser Brothers. The bad guys sometimes pulled ahead,
but there was always a good guy in the wings, ready to run out
and clock someone with a chair or throw them over the side or
slap them into a figure four, all in the name of what was right.

As I watched, I realized that Mira probably *did* know it was all
faked; she had to. But there was something satisfying about
watching the Bruiser Brothers reduced to limping off the mat,
heads in their hands, paying for what they'd done. It restored
your faith. And it was enough to push aside your skepticism and
just believe, if only for a little while, that good always wins out
in the end.

○

"The thing is," Morgan said, scooping out another measure of coffee and dumping it into a filter, "Mira has *always* been different."

We were at work, before opening, and I'd told her what had happened at the post office. She'd just sighed and nodded, as if she wasn't really surprised.

"I mean," she went on, "ever since she came here, people have been talking. Mira's an artist and this is a small town. It's practically natural."

I nodded. I was rolling silverware: knife, then fork, on a napkin, then the napkin pulled taut at a right angle and three tight rolls. Morgan watched me out of the corner of her eye, checking my technique, as she talked.

"I can still remember the first time I saw her. Me and Isabel were in high school, about your age, I guess. We were checkout girls at the Big Shop, and Mira came up one day on her bike, wearing some bright orange parka. She bought about six boxes of cereal. That's all she *ever* seemed to buy. I kept waiting for her to go into sugar shock, right there at my register."

I kept rolling, afraid she'd stop if I said anything.

"Anyway," she said, straightening the stack of filters, which was just slightly crooked, "after a while, she started to get involved in the community. I remember my mom took this painting class Mira taught over at the Community Center. It had been taught before by this old lady who had a rule that everyone could *only* paint flowers and animals. And then here comes Mira, talking about the human form, and perspective, and encouraging everyone to just throw the paint around and whatnot."

I smiled; that sounded like Mira.

"But the worst part was she talked the mailman, Mr. Rooter—who was about seventy, even then—into modeling for the class."

I looked up at this.

"*Nude* modeling," she added, doing another filter. "Apparently, it was quite horrifying. I mean, my mother never really recovered. She said she could never look at the mail the same way again."

"Wow," I said.

"I know," Morgan replied. "Mira never understood what all the fuss was about. But from then on, everyone already had their ideas about her. You're not rolling those tight enough."

"What?" I said, startled.

"You need to pull that napkin tighter," she said, pointing. "See how they're kind of loose and floppy?"

"Oh," I said. "Sorry."

She watched me, eyes narrowed, until I shaped up. "But Mira didn't even seem to notice that everyone was up in arms until they asked her to leave. And poor Mr. Rooter. I don't think anyone made eye contact with him for at *least* a year. The next week that class was back to flowers and puppies again. My mom painted this awful lopsided basset hound that she hung in the bathroom. It was really scary."

I wasn't quite sure what to say to that.

"So that was kind of how it started," she went on. "But there were other things, too. Like when some parents wanted to ban some books from the middle school. Mira freaked *out* about that, started showing up at school board meetings and making a real commotion. It just made people nervous, I guess."

"That's a shame, though," I said.

"Yeah, it is." She picked up one of my sloppy rolls and redid it, pulling the napkin tight. "But that's when they started getting kind of nasty toward her. Like I said, this is a small town. It doesn't take much to get a reputation."

"Those women I heard today in the post office," I said, softly, "one of them had this—"

"The baby," she finished for me, and I nodded. "That's Bea Williamson. The Williamsons are old Colby: country club, town government, big mansion overlooking the sound. She's got some kind of issue with Mira. I don't know what it is."

I wanted to tell her that sometimes there doesn't even have to be a reason. I knew from experience that no matter how much you turn things in your head, trying to make sense of them, some people just defy all logic.

"They were saying all these terrible things," I said, finishing another silverware. "You know, about the way she is."

"The way she is," Morgan repeated flatly.

"Yeah, well," I went on, not looking at her. I suddenly felt terrible for even bringing it up, as if I *was* Bea Williamson, just that shallow. "The way she dresses and all."

She absorbed this. "I don't know," she said, shrugging. "Mira's always been a free spirit, as long as I've known her. She's just Mira."

There was a crunching of gravel outside as the Rabbit pulled up, radio blasting. Isabel got out, wearing a pair of white sunglasses, and slammed the door.

"Oh, look at this," Morgan said loudly.

"I don't want to hear it," Isabel said, walking right past me, sunglasses still on, heading straight to the coffee machine.

"Where were you last night?"

Isabel pulled down the newly stocked container of filters and balanced it on her leg to pull one out. Then she slipped a bit, knocking a few onto the floor, which she stepped over as she went to start the coffee.

This, of course, sent Morgan into a snit.

"Give me that!" she snapped, grabbing the container and putting it on the counter, reaching in to repair the damage. "I just *did* these, Isabel."

I rolled silverware, keeping my head down.

"Sorry," Isabel said. The machine started gurgling, spitting out coffee, and she stretched and yawned while she watched.

"You know I was worried *sick* about you," Morgan said, reaching down to pick up the spilled filters. Just for spite she knocked Isabel's knee with the dustpan, which she already had at the ready for cleanup.

"Ow." Isabel stepped aside. "God, Morgan. You're not my mom. You don't need to be up nights waiting for me."

"I didn't even know where you were," Morgan grumbled, busily sweeping. "You didn't leave a note. You could have been—"

"Dead on the highway," Isabel finished for her, rolling her eyes at me. I looked back, surprised at even being acknowledged.

"Yes!" Morgan stood, dumped the grounds in the trash, then put the brush and dustpan neatly back into its place. "Easily. In my car, no less."

Isabel slammed her hand on the counter. "Don't start about the car, okay?"

"Well," Morgan said, raising her voice, "you shouldn't just take it like that with no notice, I mean, what if I had to be someplace? Considering you didn't tell me anything, I'd have no way of finding you . . ."

"Jesus, Morgan, if you weren't such an old woman maybe I would tell you more!" Isabel yelled. "Living with you is like having my grandmother breathing down my neck. So excuse me if I don't share all my intimate details, okay?"

Morgan flinched, as if she'd been hit. Then she turned around and busied herself with the sugars and Sweet'n Lows, segregating them with quick, jerky movements.

Isabel yanked out the coffeepot, stuck a cup under the stream, and let it fill up about halfway. Then she replaced the pot, took a sip of the coffee, and closed her eyes.

It was very quiet.

"I'm sorry," Isabel said loudly. It sounded more genuine than when she had said it to me. "I really am."

Morgan didn't say anything, but moved on to turning all the spoons right side up.

Isabel shot me a look which I knew meant *get lost,* so I stood and took the silverware and napkins into the kitchen. But I could still see them through the food window. I hopped up on the prep table, trying to be quiet, and watched.

"Morgan," Isabel said, softer this time. "I said I was sorry."

"You're always sorry," Morgan said without turning around.

"I know," Isabel replied, in that same low voice.

Another silence, except for Morgan arranging straws.

"I didn't even know I was going out," Isabel said. "Jeff just called and said we should go sailing so I went and then the afternoon just turned into night and the next thing I knew . . ."

Morgan turned around, her eyes wide. "Jeff? That guy we met at the Big Shop?"

"Yes," Isabel said. Now she smiled. "He called. Can you believe it?"

"Oh, my God!" Morgan said, grabbing her by the hand. "What did you do? Did you freak?"

"I had, like, totally forgotten who he was," Isabel told her, laughing. I was so used to her scowling that it took me by surprise. She looked like a different person. "He had to remind me. Can you believe that? But he's so nice, Morgan, and we spent this awesome day. . . ."

"Okay, go back, go back," Morgan said, walking around the counter and sitting down, settling in. "Start with him calling."

"Okay," Isabel said, pouring herself some more coffee. "So the phone rings. And I'm, like, in my bathrobe, watching the soaps . . ."

I stood there, listening with Morgan while Isabel told the whole story, from the call to the afternoon sail to the kiss. They'd forgotten I was even there. As Isabel acted out her date, both of them laughing, I stayed in the kitchen, out of sight, and pretended she was telling me, too. And that, for once, I was part of this hidden language of laughter and silliness and girls that was, somehow, friendship.

The two of them fascinated me. I spent most nights, after wrestling and Mira's early bedtime, sitting on the roof outside my window. I had a perfect view of the little white house from there.

Morgan and Isabel loved music. Any kind, really; from disco to oldies to Top Forty, there was always something playing in their shared background. Isabel couldn't seem to function without it. The first thing Morgan did when we got to work was start the iced tea machine; Isabel would turn on the radio and crank it up.

If Isabel was happy, she played oldies, especially Stevie Wonder's *Greatest Hits, Volume One.* If she wasn't happy, she usually put on *Led Zeppelin IV,* which Morgan hated; she called it stoner music, and it reminded her of some old boyfriend. Their CD collection, which I'd glimpsed just once as I'd stood on the front porch waiting for Morgan, was enormous. It was spread across their entire house, stacked on speakers and the TV and the coffee tables and just everywhere, spilling across the floor to make a path from one room to another.

Morgan saw me notice this. She had to kick two CDs—George Jones and Talking Heads, it looked like—out of the way just to shut the door.

"It's the Columbia Record and Tape club," she said simply, nodding toward the house. "Twelve for a penny. They hate us."

Apparently Isabel and Morgan were engaged in a mail war with Columbia, sending angry letters back and forth. But the music kept on coming. It was Isabel's main accessory as she dashed in late to work, always with two or three CDs, usually new, tucked under her arm.

At night, when I crawled out on my rooftop, it was what I heard first, rising from their windows. Usually they were on the front porch with the door propped open, the two of them lit up from behind. Isabel smoked and they split a six-pack, sitting barefoot facing each other. Every so often one of them would get up and go inside to change the music, and the other would complain.

"Don't play that Celine Dion crap again," I heard Isabel call out one night, stubbing out her cigarette. "I don't care how much you miss Mark."

Morgan reappeared in the doorway, hand on her hip. Behind her, Celine was already singing. "It was my pick, you know."

"Y'all need a new song," Isabel grumbled. "Just for that, I'm putting Zeppelin on for my next three choices."

"Isabel," Morgan said, plopping down beside her. "Then I'd have to do Neil Diamond, and you don't want that." Morgan loved crooners: Tony Bennett, Tom Jones, Frank Sinatra. She only played Frank, though, when she'd had a crappy night and was really missing Mark. I knew this music well because my mother was a Sinatra fan too.

"Well, then," Isabel said, *"I'd* have to play one of those Rush songs with a ten-minute drum solo. I wouldn't want to, but I'd have to."

"Okay," Morgan said. "I promise I'll only play this once tonight. I just miss him, that's all."

Isabel didn't say anything. She hardly ever did when Mark came up; his name always made her twist her mouth a little bit tighter and turn away.

Celine Dion kept singing, and Morgan brushed her bare foot across the porch, back and forth, mouthing the words. They didn't say anything for a while. When the song faded, Morgan

73

stuck out her bottle, and Isabel leaned forward, clinking hers against it.

This was always the truce.

If one or the other didn't have plans they'd stay out there all night. As it got later they'd get lazy and stop changing the music, letting one CD run its course. Isabel always sang along; she knew the words to everything.

I was amazed that they had so much to talk about. From the second they saw each other, there was constant laughing and sarcasm and commentary, something connecting them that pulled taut or fell limp with each thought spoken. Their words, like the music, had the potential to be endless.

chapter six

Mira had a thing for astrology. She started each morning by
reading her horoscope very carefully, then made predictions
about the day.

"Listen to this," she called out as I spread fat-free cream
cheese across my bagel. She was halfway through a big bowl of
Cap'n Crunch drowning in whole milk, the kind of breakfast
that would have horrified my mother. "'Today is a five. You will
find yourself challenged, but stay calm: relax and you'll discover
you had the wiggle room you needed all along. Highlight en-
ergy, patience, faith. Capricorn involved.'"

"Hmmm," I said, which was my usual response.

"Ought to be an interesting day," she mused, taking another
heaping spoonful of cereal. "I'd better get my errands done
early."

This meant that when I set off for work, Mira rode alongside me on her bike, pedaling slowly. She was wearing leggings, a big paisley shirt, and the purple high-tops, her hair tucked under a baseball cap. And, of course, her Terminator glasses.

She always acted like she didn't notice that people were looking at her, ignoring the laughter and occasional horn beep. That was fine; I was embarrassed enough for both of us.

When we got to the Quik Stop, right across the street from the restaurant, Mira turned in by the gas pumps and came to a squeaking stop. She waved to Ron behind the counter, who smiled and went back to his paper.

"Okay," Mira said, getting off the bike and taking her pink vinyl purse from the front basket, "we need some white bread, sliced cheese . . . and what else?"

I thought for a second as a green Toyota Camry pulled up beside us. "Ummm . . . I can't remember."

"It was something," Mira said thoughtfully, pushing up her Terminator glasses. "What was it?"

The door of the Camry slammed and I heard footsteps coming around the front of the car. "Soda?"

"No, no. It wasn't that." She closed her eyes, thinking. "It was . . ."

Someone was standing behind me now.

"Milk!" Mira said suddenly, snapping her fingers. "It was milk, Colie. *That's* what it was."

"Well, Mira Sparks," I heard a woman's voice say. "Aren't you something this morning."

I didn't even have to turn around; I just glanced into the back of the Camry. Sure enough, there was that baby, in a carseat, sound asleep with its big head hanging over to one side.

"Hello, Bea," Mira said, acknowledging her. Then she hitched up her purse and said to me, "I'll see you this afternoon."

"Okay." I turned, facing Bea Williamson, who narrowed her eyes at me. I took a few slow steps, unsure whether I should leave.

Mira opened the door to the Quik Stop, then disappeared inside. Bea Williamson took the baby out of the car, settled it on one hip, and followed right behind her.

Maybe nothing more would happen. Maybe Bea would leave it at just that tone, that one question. But I had been the butt of the joke long enough to know not to put much faith in the benefit of the doubt.

I crossed the road to the Last Chance, dodging the morning traffic. But even as I chopped lettuce, the radio up full blast, I kept glancing back at the Quik Stop, wondering what was going on inside and upset with myself for not being there.

It was a Friday, about a week later, when it happened.

Fridays were usually crazy, with day-trippers and weekenders stopping in before hitting the beach. Morgan had almost every Friday off, in case Mark was in town, which left me to suffer through them with Isabel. I'd already had two large tables and at least ten small ones and it was only one-thirty.

"Your food's up," Isabel snapped. She balanced a huge tray on her shoulder, hurrying past the line of people still waiting to be seated.

"How's it going out there?" Norman asked as I started traying my food. The music on the kitchen CD box was Stevie Wonder, loud. Isabel had been in a good mood that morning. Norman had on his green sunglasses and was grooving out at the fryer, with Bick making salads and humming behind him.

"Crazy," I told him. "At least three tables waiting."

"Four or more," Isabel said from behind me, reaching around to grab a side of fries. "I need that burger, Norman," she said, leaning closer to the window. "Pronto."

I stepped aside and Norman raised his eyebrows, smiling. He had kind of grown on me. He might have been an art freak, but he was a *sweet* art freak: he always remade my food quickly, even when the error was my fault, and made a point of setting aside the leftover bags of low-fat potato chips, which he knew I loved. On slow nights when we closed together we'd stand, him on his side of the food window, me on mine, and just talk. Days I worked with Isabel he was my only ally, but from the kitchen he couldn't do much.

"This is yours," Isabel said, pulling the rest of my order and dropping it on my tray. "You need to get this stuff *out,* not leave it sitting there getting cold and taking up space."

"I was getting it. But then you—"

"I don't give a crap." She didn't even turn around. "Just do your job, okay? That's all I'm asking."

"I am," I said, with that hot frustrated feeling I always got around her.

"Look, Morgan's not here to coddle you today," she snapped, grabbing the burger Norman handed her. "And I don't have time to explain how life is like coffee or whatever. Just stay out of my way and do your own shit." And with that she picked her tray, bumped me aside again with her hip, and was gone.

I just stood there. Every time this happened I thought up a great response—about three hours *later,* which didn't help much. Waitressing may have forced me to be braver with strangers, but Isabel was different.

"Colie, she's just like that," Norman said, like he always did. No matter how busy he was, Norman somehow noticed *everything.* I'd look up in the middle of a rush to see his eyes on me, just keeping track of where I was. It was strangely reassuring. "She doesn't—"

"I know," I said, taking a deep breath and turning back to my tables. I ran my food out and kept working, my fake smile plastered across my face. I lost myself in the buzz and busyness, avoiding Isabel until two-thirty, when things had slowed down. Then, as my last table left, I took off my apron and went out the back door.

I sat on the steps facing the Dumpsters and let my feet dangle down. In the afternoons it was sunny and bright enough to make you squint, and if the wind was blowing the right way you couldn't even smell the garbage.

A car pulled up out front and I heard the bell ring as someone came in. I looked at my watch: one minute to close. Through the back screen I could just see two girls leaning against the counter.

I started to get up but Isabel was there first, pulling a pen out of her hair. She had that snippy look on her face, like she was just waiting for these two to make her mad. "Can I help you?"

"We need takeout," one of the girls said. "Um, two cheese-burgers and an order of onion rings. And two Diet Pepsis."

"Two cheeseburgers," Isabel called out to Norman, stabbing the ticket on the spindle. "Be a few minutes," she told the girls. Then she walked towards the back door, glanced at me, and went in to the bathroom. From the kitchen I could still hear Stevie Wonder, jaunty and cheerful.

I closed my eyes, letting the sun warm my face. I could smell those cheeseburgers, and my stomach grumbled. I'd stuck to my Kiki Food Plan for the most part, with just a few french fries and onion rings here and there. Still, I was always tempted. "One day down, one victory won," my mother would say. It was the name of her best-selling inspirational tape.

I heard someone coming down the hallway and I turned, thinking it was Isabel. But it wasn't. It was one of the girls from the counter, and even squinting through the screen between us I could recognize Caroline Dawes.

She saw me, too, and looked just as surprised. For some crazy reason I thought that maybe, just maybe, things would be all right. We weren't at school. We weren't even at home. We were miles away. So I smiled at her.

"Oh, my God," she said, her nose wrinkling as if she'd seen something disgusting. "What are *you* doing here?"

Sucker.

There it was, that dry spot at the back of my throat, and instantly I was fat again, my face broken out, pulling my black trenchcoat tighter to hide myself. Except I didn't have my coat, or those forty-five-and-a-half pounds. I was a wide-open target.

Then she laughed. Laughed and shook her head, stepping back from the door with one hand covering her mouth. And she ran back to the counter, her sandals making light, cheerful slap-slap-slap noises.

I turned back to the Dumpsters and closed my eyes. I could hear myself breathing.

"Who was that?" her friend asked as she got closer.

"Colie Sparks," Caroline said. She was still laughing.

"Who?"

"She's this girl, from my school. She is like, the biggest *loser.*" Caroline was talking loudly, loud enough for me to hear all the way across the restaurant. I knew Norman could hear her, too, could imagine what he was thinking, but I wouldn't let myself turn around. "She will sleep with *anyone,* I swear to God. They call her Hole in One." She laughed again.

"That's awful," her friend said, but I could tell she was smiling by her voice.

"She totally deserves it," Caroline said. "She's the biggest slut in our school. Plus she thinks she's so cool because her mom is Kiki Sparks. Like that impresses anyone."

I pulled my legs up against my chest, balancing my chin on my knees. I could have been back at school, in the locker room, the day Caroline and her friends opened up my gym bag and took out my big panties for everyone to see.

Every time I'd thought it couldn't get worse, I was wrong.

If I'd been Mira, I would have pretended to ignore it altogether. If I'd been Morgan, I would have stood up and walked in there to give Caroline a piece of my mind. If I'd been Isabel,

I probably would have thrown a punch. But I was just me. So I pulled myself tighter and tighter, closed my eyes, and waited for it to be over.

"I just can't believe she's here," Caroline said. "If I have to see her ugly face again it'll, like, *ruin* my vacation."

Then I heard something behind me, in the hallway. Something close.

I turned around, my eyes blurring as they adjusted to the shade. It was Isabel. She was standing on the other side of the door, arms crossed over her chest. And she was watching and listening to Caroline Dawes.

Oh, great, I thought. *Now she can hate me for a reason.*

I waited for her to say something, one of those snarky, half-grumbled Isabel remarks. But she didn't. After a few seconds, Norman yelled that the order was up, and she walked back down the hallway.

I heard her ringing up their food, the drawer popping out with its cheerful *bing.* She made change and the front door creaked as Caroline or her friend pushed it open.

"There you go," I heard Isabel say. "Y'all have a good day."

"You too," Caroline's friend said, and the bell rang again as they left. Isabel came out from behind the counter and flipped the sign to CLOSED.

Whatever fresh start I'd wanted, whatever I'd wished she and Norman would think of me, was gone. Isabel would take this information and run with it.

I heard her walking back toward me, taking her time, and I swallowed hard, preparing myself. She stood on the other side of the screen. I could feel her.

"Just don't say it," I said. "Okay?" Even to my own ears, my voice sounded weak and sad.

She didn't say anything for a long time. I just concentrated on the sky, memorizing the blue. And I was startled when she said, quietly, suddenly, "Come on."

"What?" I turned around. She was looking at me.

"You heard me," she said, and she took off her apron, tossed it on the counter, and started toward the front door. She didn't look back to see if I was following her. She just went. "Come on."

We walked out to the Rabbit, leaving Norman to lock up behind us. Isabel got in and fished for the key, which was on the floor.

She cranked the engine, the CD player immediately blasting. She turned it down, but not much.

I felt like I should say something.

"Look," I said, "about that girl—"

She shook her head and reached for the volume, turning it back up and drowning me out.

We must have driven back at about seventy miles an hour. Not that I could be sure; the speedometer was broken, along with the rearview mirror, which was lopsided, and the gearshift, whose missing knob had been replaced with one of those squeezy balls painted to look like the Earth. The floor and back seat were littered with lipsticks, more CD cases, *Vogue* and *Mirabella,* and about twenty pairs of sunglasses, all of which rattled from one side to the other every time we took a turn. Isabel didn't say a word as she drove; her mouth was set in a thin, hard line.

We barely slowed down when we hit the dirt road. Since my

seat belt was also broken, I just hung on to the door handle the entire way. By the time we screeched to a halt in front of the little white house, I felt like I'd knocked a couple of fillings loose.

Isabel got out, grabbing some CDs from the backseat. "Take these," she said, and I did. I watched her kick off her shoes on the porch and get the key from under a dead plant on the steps. She unlocked the door and went inside, stepping over a few magazines and discarded articles of clothing, heading for the kitchen. I stood in the doorway.

She went to the fridge, got a beer, and knocked off the cap on the side of the counter. Then she sucked some down, burped, and put a hand on her hip.

"The world," she said, "is chock full of bitchy girls."

I came inside.

It was easy to tell which side of the bedroom was Isabel's. One had its bed made, pictures straight, the clothes on the shelves folded and sorted by category and color. The other was covered, from the floor to the bed, with *stuff*. Clothes and CDs and socks and magazines and bras and empty cigarette packs, all burying and supporting each other. But the thing I noticed most was the mirror.

It was over a dressing table, and all around it, stretching out at least a foot from each side, were hundreds of faces cut from magazines. Blonde girls, brunettes, redheads, all staring out hollow-cheeked and seductive. There were girls with drastic makeup, girls with no makeup, all of them skinny, some of them smiling. They were taped up kind of slapdash, overlapping each other, spreading out like a cloud from the mirror's edges. Here and there, mixed in, you could see pictures of real people: some of Isabel and Morgan, family pictures, a couple of babies and several of smiling, good-looking boys. Next to the models, they seemed smaller, and you noticed every imperfection.

"Sit down," Isabel said, kicking aside one white sandal and a pair of shorts to pull out the chair. The dressing table itself was a sea of little bottles and containers, so covered with cosmetics that you couldn't even see the surface. I looked at myself in the mirror, surrounded by all those beautiful girls, and wondered what I was doing there.

Isabel pushed some more stuff aside and leaned against the dressing table, taking another swig of her beer. "Look, Colie. I have something to say to you, and I'm just gonna shoot it straight. Okay?"

I considered this. It couldn't be any worse than what had already happened. "Okay."

She tucked her hair behind her ear, took a deep breath and let it out. Then she said, "I really think you should pluck your eyebrows."

This hadn't been exactly what I was expecting.

"What?" I said.

"You heard me," she said, coming to stand behind me and turning my head to face my reflection. "And it wouldn't hurt to do something about that hair, either."

"I don't know," I said uncertainly as she went to the closet and yanked the door open, pulling out a large box of hair coloring kits. And here I'd thought she was a natural blonde.

"That black is just too uneven," she said. "You can't dye over it, but at least we could try to do it again and get it all. It won't

85

fix it totally, but—" She dropped the box on the floor and abruptly left the room, still talking to herself. I listened to her open and shut cabinets in the kitchen.

I looked back up at the pictures, taking in each of the faces. And then I saw it; one, stuck at the top, that I hadn't noticed before. It looked like a yearbook picture. The girl in it was fat, with glasses. She had a pudgy face and limp brown hair, and she was wearing a thick turtleneck sweater that looked really uncomfortable and itchy. She had a necklace with a little gold frog on it, something her mother or grandmother must have given her. She was the kind of girl that Caroline Dawes would have made miserable. A girl like me.

I leaned closer, wondering why she was there. Even with the pictures of the babies and Morgan and all those boys, she didn't fit in.

"Here," Isabel said, coming back into the room suddenly and dropping a box in my lap. The model on the front had dark brown hair, almost black, with a tinge of red in it, and she smiled up at me. "That's what I'm thinking."

I didn't know what Caroline Dawes had triggered in Isabel but I wasn't about to question it. After the day I'd had, any change seemed like a good idea.

"Okay," I said. And behind me, reflected in the mirror among all those other beauties, Isabel's pretty face almost, just almost, smiled.

"Ouch."
"Hush."
"Ouch!"

"Shut up."

"*Ouch!*"

"Will you please be quiet?" Isabel snapped, yanking what had to be a fair amount of skin with another pluck.

"It *hurts*," I said. She'd searched for some ice cubes, but no luck: she'd forgotten to fill the tray the night before.

"Of course it hurts," she grumbled, tipping my head further back. "Life sucks. Get over it."

Obviously, we wouldn't be best friends immediately.

To distract myself, I looked over at the mirror. "Who's that girl?"

"What girl." Another yank.

I had tears in my eyes. "That one," I said, pointing toward the chubby girl in the turtleneck. "In the yearbook picture."

She gave another good yank, then looked where I was pointing. "My cousin," she said distractedly.

"Oh."

"She's a real looker, huh." She switched the tweezers to the other hand, flexing her cramped fingers.

"Well, she's," I said, "I mean, she's very . . ."

"She's a dog," she said, settling in to start on my other brow. "It's no secret."

It was always so easy for beautiful girls. They never could understand how lucky they were. But I knew her cousin, knew what she was going through. And I couldn't take my eyes off her, even as Isabel worked to transform me.

She was finishing my eyebrows, just plucking stray hairs here and there, her face close to mine.

"Why are you being so nice to me?" I asked her.

She sat back, putting down the tweezers. "You know," she said, "when you say stuff like that I just want to slap you."

"What?"

"You heard me." She picked up her beer and took a swallow, still watching me. Then she said, "Colie, you should never be surprised when people treat you with respect. You should expect it."

I shook my head. "You don't know—" I began. But, as usual, she didn't let me finish.

"Yes," she said simply, "I do know. I've watched you, Colie. You walk around like a dog waiting to be kicked. And when someone does, you pout and cry like you didn't deserve it."

"No one deserves to be kicked," I said.

"I disagree," she said flatly. "You do if you don't think you're worth any better. As soon as you saw that girl today you crumpled. You just opened the door up and let her stomp right in."

I thought of Mira, how much it bothered me that she hadn't fought back. "She's—"

"I don't care *who* she is," she said, waving her hand as she interrupted me, *again*. "Self-respect, Colie. If you don't have it, the world will walk all over you."

I looked down, running my tongue over my piercing.

"See," she said, "you're doing it again."

"I am not."

She lifted my chin so I had to look at her. "It's all about *you*, Colie." She touched one finger to her temple, *tap tap tap*. "Believe in yourself up here and it will make you stronger than you could ever imagine."

There is something infectious about confidence. And for that one moment, with my eyebrows burning and my eyes watering, I believed.

"And good hair never hurt either," she said, grabbing the dye box off the floor. "Come on. I've got plans later but if we hurry we can get this done now."

I just sat there, peering in the mirror at my reflection. One small change, but I looked different already.

"Let's go!" she yelled from the kitchen. I took one last look at myself, framed by all those beautiful girls, and went to put myself in her hands. But when she sat me down in a kitchen chair and tipped my head back over the sink, telling me to close my eyes, I could think only of that one girl, her dorky fat cousin, as the water splashed all around me.

chapter seven

I was on my way home when I bumped into Norman.

Literally. I was walking backward, waving good-bye to Isabel, when I crashed into something solid.

"Mmmpht," it said, and there was a thump and a clatter. I turned around to see Norman, lying underneath a huge painting with only his feet and head sticking out. He blinked at me.

"Hi," he said.

"Hi." I was alarmed. "Are you okay?"

"Oh, yeah," he said easily, carefully moving the canvas and sitting up. It was a strange night, balmy, with the wind coming off the water in a curvy kind of breeze. My shorts were flapping against my legs and everything smelled like rain. "I'm fine."

"I'm sorry," I said.

"Don't be." He stood up, flexing one of his wrists, which

cracked. He was wearing a T-shirt that said CAN'T STOP DANCING! in worn, white letters. "I was just going to drop this off," he said, nodding toward the canvas.

"What is it?" I said. The breeze blew across us again, ruffling the trees. I could hear thunder off somewhere, a low grumble like someone clearing his throat.

"Oh, just this painting I did," he said. "It's part of a series."

"You paint, too?"

"Yeah." He tipped it back and looked at it, then rested it against his legs again. "Well, my best stuff is this kind of object sculpture. I'm really into bicycle gears right now. But I've been working on this series of paintings for my portfolio for art school. It's kind of experimental. This one's of Isabel and Morgan." He turned it around so I could see.

They were both in sunglasses. Morgan's pair was red and cat's-eye shaped, with black edging; Isabel's, big and white, took up half her face. They were sitting at the counter at the Last Chance. Morgan was resting her chin on her hand, and Isabel had her lips pursed, as if she was about to blow a kiss. Even if I hadn't known them, I would have understood they were close. All they were was right there to see.

"This is great," I said. He shuffled his feet. "I'm *serious*, Norman."

"Well, it's okay," he said in his lazy way, turning it so he could look at it again. "I'm really interested in the idea of anonymity and familiarity. And sunglasses, you know, are so indicative of that. I mean, they're worn by some people to hide themselves. But they're also a fashion statement, meant to be noticed. So there's a dichotomy there."

I just looked at him. Even after a month of knowing and working and talking with Norman, this was the longest, most complicated thing I'd ever heard him say.

"Norman," I said, as the thunder rumbled closer, "that's amazing."

He smiled. "Yeah, it's pretty cool. It got me into art school, anyway. Now I just have to finish the series." He picked up the painting again. "I only have three so far. But I promised when I finished this one I'd bring it over so they could see it."

I remembered, suddenly, the portrait of Mira and Cat Norman that hung in the living room.

There was a loud boom right behind us, over the water, and I heard Mira's front door fly open and slam shut in the wind.

We both looked up toward the house, lit up yellow and bright in the increasing darkness. And then I saw Mira slipping past window after window, her hands pressed against her face.

"What's going on?" I said, but Norman was already halfway up the lawn, the canvas banging against his leg. There was another clap and it started to rain, hard, splattering my bare arms.

"Cat Norman!" I heard Mira call out as we came up onto the porch, the door still swinging and banging in the wind. "Where are you?"

"Mira," I yelled, grabbing the door to silence it. "What's wrong?"

"I can't find him!" she yelled back. The wind was blowing through an open window on the porch, a few loose papers whirling past. "Cat Norman!"

"It's okay," Norman said. "He's around here somewhere."

She stepped into the doorway of the back room, her hair

sticking out around her head. "I could hear him a few minutes ago, but now . . . you know how he's scared of storms."

I jumped at another thunderclap: it was *close*. "Stay there," I said, as Norman rested his painting against the front bay window, out of the rain. "We'll find him."

"Damn cat," she grumbled, disappearing from sight again.

"Cat Norman!" Norman called from the other side of the porch. "Here, boy!"

"Where is he?" Mira said as she passed a second time. "It's that dog again, I know it. . . ."

"He's got to be around here somewhere," I told her. "Don't worry." And then I stepped back outside.

It was pouring, the treetops swaying back and forth. Isabel was out on the porch of the little white house, watching the storm roll in across the water.

"Cat Norman," I said, peering under the bushes. The grass was wet and stuck to my feet. "Here, boy. Come on."

"*Nor*-man," I heard Norman yelling, around the other side.

"*Nor*-man," I repeated.

Lightning hit close enough to shake the ground beneath me and flicker the lights in the house, and I was beginning to think Cat Norman would have to ride this one out alone when I met up with Norman in the backyard. He'd been checking his room.

"We should go in," he said. There was a flash, another big bang, and above us the birdfeeders, swinging madly in the wind, rained down a shower of sunflower seeds.

"He's probably under the house," I told him as we ran up the back steps, the rain hard on my shoulders. We huddled under the slim awning and I reached for the knob. It was locked.

"Shoot," Norman said.

"Mira," I yelled, banging on it. "Open the door." The wind came up hard behind us, blowing rain and birdseed against my legs.

No answer. I knew she was probably at the front of the house, peering into the bushes by the steps, Cat Norman's favorite hiding spot. The open windows had let in enough wind to blow almost everything off the table: napkins were circling in midair, placemats scattered colorful and bright across the floor. I could have tried to force the door, but knew well that the LOCK STICKS OCCASIONALLY.

"Mira," I repeated, shouting. "Open up, okay?"

"She can't hear us," Norman said.

I kept banging as the rain came harder, stinging now, and the windchimes next to my head, clanging crazily, left their nail altogether and flew off into the yard, still singing.

"Mira." I pressed my hand against the glass as the wind pushed me against the house. "Come *on*."

"We have to make a run for the front door," Norman said in my ear. "Are you ready?"

I turned around. It was raining so hard I couldn't even see the water, just a blurred gray wall in front of me.

"Ready?" Norman said. He glanced at me.

"I—" I said, swallowing hard.

"Set?" Norman said.

Another flash of lightning, and I knew to wait, to hold my breath for what would follow.

"*Go!*" he shouted, grabbing my hand and yanking me down

the stairs, just as a huge *boom* rose out of the darkness in front of us. I think I screamed.

We ran right into the noise, the ground shaking as my feet touched it, but we kept going, his hand laced tight in mine. I could feel rain against my eyes, in my mouth, splashing in my ears.

When we ran up onto the front porch, soaked, I was completely out of breath. I leaned against the door and closed my eyes.

Norman was still holding my hand, his palm warm against mine.

"Man," he said. He was grinning, but shakily. "That was *intense*."

"I can't believe we made it," I said.

He smiled, then looked down at our hands. I let go, quickly, without even thinking.

Norman slid his hand into his pocket.

I felt something. Something wet and hairy, brushing across my leg with slow, ambling laziness.

"Meow," Cat Norman said simply, parking his big butt by my foot and looking up at me. "Meow."

"I hate you," I told him. He didn't flinch.

"Dumb cat," Norman said, reaching down to scoop him up. He opened the door and dropped him inside.

The wind was dying down now, the rain reduced to a constant stream, rattling through the gutters and overflowing the drainpipe. I was sure Cat Norman had already found his way to Mira's side, to be gathered up in her arms and forgiven, as always.

"Well," Norman said suddenly.

"Well," I said.

He leaned closer to me, squinting. "You look different," he pronounced. "Don't you?"

I touched a hand to my dripping hair, remembering my afternoon in Isabel's hands. "Yeah," I said. "I guess I do."

He nodded, smiling. "It looks good," he told me, in that slow, earnest way of his. "It does."

"Thanks." All I could think of was him holding my hand, tight, as we ran into the storm. Hippie Norman. *So* not the guy for me. But still.

Stop it, I told myself. No matter how nice he was acting, he'd heard what Caroline Dawes had said. Of course he wanted to hold my hand. And do everything else that you do with girls like me.

"I have to go in," I said abruptly.

"Oh, right," he said quickly, a bit surprised. He glanced at the painting. "I guess I'll just take this over later, when it stops raining."

"Okay," I said. " 'Bye, Norman."

"Yeah. Uh, 'bye." And he started backing off the porch, down the steps. " 'Bye," he called again when he was halfway across the yard.

I went in and shut the door. He'd only grabbed my hand out of instinct, to pull me along. I knew that.

But I waited, watching him until he was out of sight, before I turned and went up the stairs.

Mira was in her room with Cat Norman; I could hear her alternately cooing and chastizing him. I closed the windows in the back room, gathering up the papers and placemats, then turned off a few lights and went outside to retrieve the windchimes from the birdbath, where they'd landed. The inside of the house felt unsteady and loose, like it had been breathing hard, all the pent-up air pushed out and away.

In Mira's studio, cards were strewn everywhere, some open, some shut. As I collected them I read each one, each separate way of saying *I'm sorry . . .*

. . . for your loss, for it is hard to lose one who added so much.

. . . for he was a good man, a good father, and a good friend.

. . . from all of us who worked with her, and whose lives she touched.

. . . he was a friend and companion, and I will miss seeing you two walking each morning together.

Dead ex-husbands, dead co-workers, even dead dogs. Thousands of apologies over the years.

I dried myself off and fixed some soup, then sat down to watch wrestling, out of habit, alone, as Mira moved around upstairs, running water for her nightly bath. Rex Runyon and Lola Baby had reconciled, but there were already problems. The Sting Ray and Mr. Marvel's partnership was being sorely tested by several ongoing defeats to Tiny and Whitey, and during a match between some unknown and the Swift Snake the referee was thrown completely out of the ring onto the ground, landing with a crash. And the crowd roared.

During a commercial I flipped a few channels and found my mother: some news program was covering her antifat crusade through Europe. She was in London now. On TV my mother looked even better than in person: her skin glowed, her smile was broad. For the first time I realized how similar she and Mira were—the way they waved their hands around excitedly while they talked, drawing you in.

"So, Kiki," said the interviewer, a round-faced Englishman with a clipped accent, "I understand you have a new philosophy you're speaking about on this trip."

"That's right, Martin!" my mother replied cheerily in her go-go-go infomercial voice. "I'm speaking to everyone out there who sees themselves as a caterpillar, but knows that somewhere in them lives a butterfly."

"A caterpillar?" Martin looked skeptical.

"Yes." My mother leaned forward, fixing her eyes on him. She said, "There are a lot of people out there, Martin, who are watching this as they've watched a million other fitness shows and infomercials, longing for results. But they're caterpillars, watching butterflies. And there's a crucial step in there. They still have to *become*."

"Become." Martin shifted his clipboard to the other leg.

"Become," my mother repeated. "And that's where I come in. I am the work between those caterpillars and this world of butterflies. They all have the potential. It's been there all along. They just have to *become*."

And there was that sparkle in her eye, bright enough to reach across an ocean and still get me. My mother believed, and she could make you do it, too. She'd believed me all the way out of forty-five-and-a-half pounds. She'd believed us from living out of the car to having anything we wanted. And now, she would believe millions of people from depressed, Burger King–scarfing caterpillars into gorgeous, thin, brightly colored butterflies.

Later, as I put away the dishes, I caught a glimpse of myself in the window: my hair different, the new shape of my eyebrows affecting my entire face. *A work in progress,* Isabel had allowed as she stood back and admired what she'd done. I'd been a caterpillar for so long, and although I had shed my cocoon in losing my fat, my coat, and the years that led me here, I wasn't a butterfly yet. For now, all I could do was stand on the ground and look up at the sky, not quite ready yet to leap and rise.

chapter eight

As the weeks passed, I got somewhat more used to being with Mira in public. The bike didn't bother me much anymore, or the clothes, unless she was really suited up, which was rare enough so that it was ultimately avoidable. It was the reaction of the rest of the world—the rest of Colby—that remained hard to take.

It wasn't just Bea Williamson, of course. There were the women at the library who rolled their eyes when they saw Mira coming. The men at the hardware store who stifled their laughter as she picked intently through the screw section, pink purse tucked under her arm. Some people just smirked, ducking their heads. But others made it clear how they felt.

"So, Mira," a man had said at the drugstore, where we were buying Super Glue for more fix-it projects, "the annual Fourth of July church bazaar is coming up soon. I'm sure we can count on you to be a star customer, can't we?"

Or at the supermarket, in a hushed whisper from a pack of women huddled by the frozen foods, while Mira chose some cookies: "My goodness, Mira Sparks certainly does like those sweets, doesn't she? And it *shows*."

The fat jokes, for obvious reasons, were the worst. But I didn't say anything; this wasn't my fight. And if it was killing Mira, as it would have me, she hid it well. I only wondered if one day she would break altogether from the strain of holding it all in.

The closest we'd ever come to talking about it was one day at the Quik Stop, after some woman had complimented Mira, quite snidely, on her Terminator sunglasses.

"She's not very nice," I'd said tentatively as Mira got on her bike.

But Mira had shrugged, nudging her kickstand with one foot. "Oh, now," was all she'd said, as if it was *me* that was out of line. And then she was gone, weaving back and forth across the empty road, taking her time going home.

But there were nights, after she'd gone upstairs with Cat Norman under her arm, when I'd seen the line of light under her bedroom door. I pictured her sitting on the bed, hearing those voices again in her head the way I still heard mine. If Mira was anything like me, she could only keep them out for so long. And I knew it was always late at night, when everything and everyone else was quiet, that those voices would rise like ghosts, soft and haunting, filling your mind until sleep finally came.

O

One morning on the week of the Fourth of July, Morgan burst into work with a huge grin on her face.

"Oh, my God," Isabel said. She was standing by the coffee machine, working on her third cup; it was drizzling and cool, bad beach weather, and we'd been slow. "What is it?"

"Mark's coming home tonight, for the weekend," Morgan said, almost goofy with happiness. "He just called."

"Great," Isabel said. "Ya-hoo."

"Don't be like that," Morgan scolded, coming behind the counter and adjusting the coffee cups, pointing their handles in the proper direction. Then she moved on to the napkins, replacing them on the shelf at a right angle to the spoons. But she was still smiling. "You like Mark," she told Isabel.

"Of course I do," Isabel said sarcastically. "And if he actually shows *up* this time, I'll like him even more. Besides, I thought we had plans."

"He just called and said he was coming." Morgan put a hand on her hip. There were certain postures and expressions that made her look kind of like a dodo bird. But I felt bad for thinking this.

"He said that last time, too." Isabel craned her neck, checking on her only table.

Morgan rolled her eyes, then looked at me pleadingly. "Work for me tonight, Colie? Please?"

A double. But if I owed anyone, it was Morgan. "Sure."

"Thanks." She smiled, flashing her ring as she pushed her bangs out of her face. "I have, like, a million things to do. I want to cook him dinner, you know? So I need to clean the house, and buy some food, and do something with my hair. . . ."

Isabel turned back to the coffee machine, grumbling under her breath.

"So, Is," Morgan said after a moment, "can I have the house tonight?"

"Where am I supposed to go?" Isabel said.

Morgan lowered her voice. "You know Mira would let you stay there." I pretended to have to go back into the kitchen, where I found Norman with a book by the rain-streaked window. He glanced up and smiled, then turned a page and kept reading. Bick, who was an aging surfer, was out back with his board, waxing it and looking up glumly at the gray sky.

I could still see Morgan through the food window. "Just for tonight," she said. "I want it to be . . . special."

"Oh, gag," Isabel groaned. "Whatever. I'll get lost, if that's what you want."

"You *rock*," Morgan said excitedly, running over and giving her a quick hug. Isabel just stood there. "Okay, then, I guess I should go. He's coming in around six and I have so much to talk to him about . . . I mean, we've got to set a date for the wedding. Especially if I want to go back to school in the fall, I kind of have to know when. I mean, there's so much to plan, you know?"

Isabel swirled her spoon in her cup, adding more cream and sugar. Morgan watched, her smile wavering.

"Isabel," Morgan said. "Don't be like this. I never get to see him."

"Did he say anything about last time?" Isabel snapped. She had her back to me now. I leaned in closer against the cooler door, easing out of sight. "Did he at least *apologize?*"

"I didn't ask him to—"

"Did he say he was sorry you waited up for him all night and that he stood up your entire family? Did he explain why he never picked up the phone to call you?"

"That isn't important now."

Isabel shook her head angrily. "God, Morgan. You are such a smart girl. Why are you being so *stupid* about this?"

Morgan blinked, several times. And bit by bit, that grin just slipped off her face. "It's none of your business," she said quietly.

"It isn't?"

"No." She turned and walked out from behind the counter, grabbing her keys. "It isn't."

"Then don't cry to me anymore, okay?" Isabel yelled after her. I heard the bell over the front door. "Don't sob and say how much he's hurt you and make a big deal of taking off the ring and taking down his pictures. 'Cause I'm sick of it. So it's none of my business. Not anymore."

The door slammed. Isabel turned back to the window, angrily stirring her coffee. Then she saw me.

"What?" she snapped.

I shook my head. Across the kitchen, Norman kept reading, like a child so used to his parents fighting he hardly heard it anymore. And Isabel dumped her coffee and walked to the back door, where she stood watching the rain, arms across her chest, until her table was ready to leave.

That night, Isabel was off first, around nine, so Norman and I closed up together.

"Want a ride?" he asked as we stepped out into the parking lot. I could hear his keys jingling as he locked the door.

"Are you going home?" I said.

"I could." He tossed up the keys, then caught them. "I need to make some room in my place, since the church bazaar is this weekend. It's where I usually get most of my best stuff."

I thought about the walk home. All of those bright house lights, the occasional glare of high beams coming toward me, making me squint. A ride would have been nice, but now I had to wonder what Norman expected in return.

"I'm okay," I said, and started across the parking lot.

"So, I, uh, got you something," he called after me. I turned around. He was standing next to the open passenger door of his wagon, the dome light glowing. In the back seat I could see a stack of egg crates, a lamp that appeared to be shaped like a windmill, and a large plastic goldfish. Norman, the collector.

"Got me something?" I said.

"Yeah." He sat down in the passenger seat and opened the glove box; there was the ritual explosion of sunglasses. He rummaged through them quickly, glancing up a few times as if to make sure I hadn't left.

I stayed where I was.

"All right," he announced triumphantly, picking out one pair and tossing all the others back into the glove box. When he slammed it shut it fell open. Twice. And then stuck, with one good whack.

I came closer as he got out and took a few steps to meet me halfway, under the bright white of the one buzzing street lamp.

"Here." He deposited the sunglasses in my open hand; I could feel their slight weight in my palm. "I just saw them and, you know, thought of you."

Thought of me. I looked down at them. They were black, with cat's-eye-shaped frames, slim and streamlined. Very cool.

"Wow," I said. "Thanks." But I ran my tongue over my piercing to remind myself that nothing had really changed. I was still Hole in One, even as I stood under that white, white light with Norman, a cool breeze on the back of my neck.

"Well," Norman said quickly, to cover my lack of enthusiasm, "I was just at this flea market and I saw them. You know."

"I know," I said, tucking them into my shirt pocket. "Thanks."

He nodded, already retreating.

"'Bye, Norman," I called out as I reached the edge of the parking lot. He was standing by his car, keys in hand. He waved, but he didn't say anything.

I walked fast, hands in my pockets, until I heard him drive away. Then I pulled out those sunglasses. A perfect fit. I wore them all the way back to Mira's.

When I walked up to the house, Isabel was waiting.

"Hey," she called out, startling me. She was sitting in the yard, cross-legged, a beer in her hand.

"Hey," I said, keeping my voice down as I glanced up and saw the light on in Mira's room. I didn't know if she was sleeping. "What are you doing?"

She stretched back, resting on her palms. It was a nice night, good for sitting out in the grass. "Killing time," she said. "I've been displaced, you know." And she nodded over her shoulder toward the little white house. She seemed to be in a better mood.

"Oh," I said. "Right." I stepped over the row of small hedges lining the driveway to join her. She had her head tilted back, eyes closed.

I could hear music, faintly, coming from the little house. Celine Dion.

"I hate this song." Isabel took a big swig off her beer.

I didn't say anything.

"What time is it?" she asked, opening her eyes and sitting up straight.

I glanced at my watch. "Ten-fifteen."

She nodded. "Four hours and fifteen minutes late," she said in a loud voice. "And *counting.*"

The music stopped, then started again. It was the same song, from the beginning. I could see Morgan moving around inside the little house. There was a bouquet of flowers on the trunk that served as a coffee table, and it looked like all the CDs had been straightened and stacked. She seemed to still be working on it, picking things up and moving them from one side of the room to the other. Every time she passed the door she leaned into the glass, peering out toward the dark road.

"He's not coming," Isabel called out.

Morgan opened the door and stuck her head out. "I heard that," she said. Then she shut the door.

"Good," Isabel replied quietly. Morgan moved the vase of flowers to the other side of the coffee table.

Behind the house, there was a crackling noise, and a flash of light over the water. I could hear someone laughing, far off.

"It's not the Fourth of July yet, idiots," Isabel said. "It's *tomorrow*."

I looked up at Mira's house. Cat Norman was sitting in her window. Mira was on her bed, in her kimono, hands in her lap. Her hair was down and she was barefoot. Just staring.

I wondered if she could see us.

"It's not that I don't want Morgan to be happy," Isabel said, as another set of fireworks went off in the distance. "Because I do. But he doesn't make her happy."

"She loves him," I pointed out.

"She doesn't know any better." She finished her beer, depositing it in the six-pack behind her.

Morgan sat down on the couch. She moved the flowers again.

"He's the only one who's ever told her she was beautiful," Isabel said. "And she's afraid she'll never hear it from anyone else."

Upstairs, Mira had gotten off the bed and walked toward the window, leaning over Cat Norman.

I reached up to brush my hair out of my eyes and realized I still had on Norman's sunglasses. When I took them off the moon seemed even brighter.

"Those are nice," Isabel said.

"Thanks."

"Norman must like you."

"Oh, no," I said quickly. "He just found them at some flea market."

"I don't mean he *likes* you," she said, drawing the word out. "He's just very picky about people." She reached around for another beer. "You should be flattered."

"Yeah," I said. "I am." Now I wished I'd taken the ride, or thanked him more.

Isabel popped the top off the bottle, running her finger around the neck. "Who was that girl, yesterday?" she asked. "The one who said those things about you."

I looked up at Mira's room. She'd moved back to the end of the bed and had Cat Norman in her arms. As she petted him his tail twitched back and forth, back and forth.

"Just this girl from school."

"She thought she knew you pretty well."

"She hates me," I said.

"Why?"

I looked down at the grass, brushing my fingers across it. I could feel her waiting for me to answer. "I don't know."

"Must be a reason."

"No," I said. "There isn't." She might have wanted more, but that was all she was getting, for now.

She sighed. "High school sucks," she said finally. "It gets better."

I looked at her: perfect figure, perfect hair, gorgeous and self-confident. If I looked like Isabel, no one could touch me. "Yeah, right," I said. "Like you know about that."

"What's that supposed to mean?"

"Girls like you," I said, "don't even know how bad it is."

"Girls like me," she repeated. And she kind of half smiled, as if I'd said something funny. "What kind of girl am I, Colie?"

I shook my head. In the little house, Morgan sat down on the couch again. Morgan would understand this. She'd been like me, once, I knew it.

"Tell me," Isabel said, leaning closer. "Go ahead."

"A pretty one. Smart," I said. "Popular. You were probably even a cheerleader, for God's sake." I felt stupid now, but it was too late to stop. "You were the kind of girl that never knew what it was like to have someone treat you the way that girl treated me. You have no idea."

She watched me as I said this, her face smooth and calm. I could see her in high school, with a boyfriend in a varsity jacket, wearing little skirts that swirled around her perfect legs. I could see her at the prom, with a tiara and an armful of flowers. And I could see her in the gym locker room, taunting a girl who was fat and dorky with no friends. A girl like me.

"You're wrong," she said quietly, leaning back again.

"Yeah, right," I said. She could have been Caroline Dawes then, for all the anger I felt simmering in me. "Then what were you?"

"I was afraid," she said. And she turned her head away, looking back at the bright lights of the little house. "Just like you."

We sat there for a moment, watching Morgan move through the living room.

"It's so, so stupid," she added softly, "what we do to ourselves because we're afraid. It's so *stupid*." And she kept her head turned, as if I wasn't even there.

But she was wrong. She wasn't anything like me, and I was so close, again, to telling her why. To telling her everything. But just as I started, she turned back and I lost my nerve.

I thought of my mother, suddenly, of all those caterpillars

waiting to Become. Of Mira, pretending to ignore the taunts that followed her. Of Morgan with her square face and lover's grin. And me and Isabel, under a big yellow moon.

Isabel didn't move when the car passed Mira's driveway and pulled up in front of the little house. She didn't turn around as someone got out of the car and strode up those stairs, Morgan running to meet him halfway. And she didn't say a word as they went inside, the lights clicking off behind them and leaving us in the dark, with only that moon and the light from Mira's window to see our way back.

chapter nine

The next morning, the real Fourth of July, I woke up early to go for a run, leaving Isabel crashed on the sofa. I could hear the floor creaking overhead as Mira got dressed and collected Cat Norman.

On my way down the path I passed by Norman's door. It was ajar and I decided to stop in and thank him for the sunglasses after all. When I knocked, the door fell open. The room was *packed:* canvases lined the walls, stacked against each other, and hanging from the ceiling were at least ten mobiles, all of them shifting in the breeze coming in behind me. They were made of odds and ends, bits and pieces: bicycle gears, old Superballs, tiny framed pictures cut out of magazines. One was just made up of old metal rulers and protractors, clinking against each other. The mannequins he'd carried in on my first day were leaning against the wall, their midsections painted wild colors, arms stretched out, fingers Day-Glo and cheerful. The bazaar was tomorrow; I couldn't imagine where he could fit anything else.

I found Norman in the corner on a futon, asleep under a mobile of different-colored sunglasses parts. The room was cold and he was murmuring, shirtless, the sheets tangled around him. I couldn't take my eyes off him: his face was flushed, one arm thrown over a pillow, fingers brushing the wall. He looked *different* to me somehow, like some other guy, one I'd never met. And I felt strange, as if he might at any moment open his eyes and I'd have to explain myself, standing there without the food window or a shared purpose safely between us. I backed away quickly, bumping against a mannequin on the way out. But I wondered for my entire run what he'd been dreaming.

The beach was cool and misty, and as I ran I kept thinking of Mira, too, remembering what Isabel had said the night before. *What we do to ourselves because we're afraid.*

I knew one person whom I saw as mostly fearless. And I knew she was the only one who might understand.

"Colie?" I could hear the phone jostling around as she sat up in bed. "What's wrong?"

"Nothing," I said. "I just wanted to talk to you."

My mother was in Spain. I'd had to go through three operators, two hotel clerks and one new, irritated assistant to get to her. "I miss you," I told her. It was always easier to say it over the phone.

"Oh, honey." She sounded surprised. "I miss you, too. How's everything?"

"Good." I pulled the phone further into the kitchen and sat down on the floor. I filled her in on my job, and Isabel doing my hair and eyebrows; I was surprised at how much had happened since we'd last talked. She told me about signing autographs for three hours, how rich the food was in Europe, and how she'd had to fire yet another assistant for being argumentative, could I believe *that*.

Finally, I got to the real reason I'd called.

"Mom."

"Yes?"

"Did you know Mira's, well . . . a little eccentric?" I whispered, even though she was upstairs.

"What?" My mother was still steamed about the assistant.

"Mira," I repeated. "She's not like I remembered her. She's kind of . . . out there."

"Oh goodness," my mother said. "Well, Mira always had that artistic sensibility."

"It's more than that," I said. "People here . . . they're kind of mean to her."

"Oh," she said. "Well, I knew she'd had some run-ins with the locals. . . ."

"I know about that."

"Oh." She paused. I could see her on the other end of the line, biting her lip in thought. "Well, Mira has always been Mira. I never realized it was that serious."

"I wish we had," I said. "I just feel so bad . . ."

"Oh, Colie, I am so *sorry*," she said, talking over me. "I

feel just awful about this trip and leaving you anyway, and now this. . . . Look. I'll just send Amy, my assistant, home to Charlotte on the next flight. You can take the train back and just stay with her while I finish up this tour."

"Mom," I said. "No. Wait."

But she wasn't listening, already had her hand cupped over the receiver, while she called to someone in the room. "Look into flights back home, will you. . . ."

"Mom."

". . . Today or tomorrow would be best. And tell Amy . . ."

"Mom!"

". . . that she should pack and call the cleaning service, plus book a train ticket—"

"Mom!"

I had to yell. Once my mother set something in motion, there was no stopping her.

"What!" she yelled back. "Colie, just a second, okay?"

"No," I said. "I don't want to go home. I'm fine here."

Another pause. I pictured people still scurrying in Spain, planning my instant departure. "Are you sure?"

"I'm sure." I switched the phone to my other ear. "I'm having fun and I like my job. And I think Mira likes having me here. I just feel bad for her. That's all."

"Well," she said hesitantly. "Okay. But if you feel the situation is getting too strange, you call me and I will send someone. Okay?"

"Okay," I said, as I heard her tell someone not to bother, everything was fine. "I promise."

She sighed. "Poor Mira," she said. "You know, she always had

115

a hard time with people. Even when we were kids. She was just different."

"Not like you," I said.

"Oh, I had my hard times," she said easily. This was comfortable territory for her; the hard times were what made her Kiki Sparks. "But it was different with Mira. People have always had difficulty really *understanding* her."

"Mom?"

"Yeah." When it was just the two of us, she'd eventually drop most of her Kiki-ness and become my mom again. But you always had to give it a while.

"Were you," I asked hesitantly, "were you always so brave?"

There was a pause as she absorbed this. "Brave?" she said. "Me?"

"Come on," I told her. "You know you are."

She thought about it for a second. "I don't think of myself as brave, Colie. You don't remember how hard we had it in the Fat Years. And I'm glad for that. I wasn't always so strong."

I did remember. But she didn't need to know that.

"You know what I think it is?" she said suddenly. I could hear her moving around and I pictured her in the hotel bed, pillows fluffed behind her. "I think that losing the weight was a big part of it, me starting to be unafraid. But more, I think it was when other people really started to believe in me. All those women who looked to me to be strong and capable for them, to show them the way. So I faked it."

"You faked it," I repeated slowly.

"Yeah, I did. But then, somehow," she went on, "somewhere

along the way, I started to believe it myself. I think that be-ing brave and self-confident doesn't necessarily start inside, honey. It starts with the rest of the world, and it leads back to you."

The rest of the world, I thought. *Okay.*

"Why are you asking?" my mother said, suddenly suspicious. "What's going on?"

"Nothing," I said. "I just wondered. That's all."

I was at the table eating cereal when Mira came downstairs. I could hear her in the kitchen, opening cabinets and starting cof-fee and talking to Cat Norman, who eventually found his way to me and leapt up on to the table, knocking my spoon out of the bowl and splattering milk everywhere.

"You think you're so smart, don't you," I said as he bent his head to lap it up, his tongue scratching against the tabletop.

"Good morning!" Mira said cheerfully as she came through the door, carrying an overflowing bowl of Trix, the paper tucked under her arm. "How are you?"

"Good," I said, nodding toward the paper. "What's your day looking like?"

"Ah!" she said, putting down her bowl. She unfolded the pa-per, smoothing it out on the table. "'Today is a seven.' Ooh, that's good." She cleared her throat. "'A day for solitude and quiet: you have a lot to think about. Recycling, renewal, big things to come are on your mind.'"

"Wow," I said.

"I know." She scanned the page. "And your day is a four. Listen to this: 'Sometimes, words are louder than actions. Keep your eyes open. Pisces involved.' "

"Hmmmm."

She turned in her chair, glancing at the calendar behind her. "So for me, 'Big things to come' has got to be that lunar eclipse . . . or maybe the church bazaar?"

"Or the Fourth of July," I offered.

"Pssh," she said. "Not my kind of holiday: lots of tourists, too noisy. I'll go with the eclipse. Or a bountiful day at the bazaar." She dug into her cereal, chewing thoughtfully.

"You know, Mira," I said, "I wonder what else you could possibly *need* at the bazaar."

She looked at me. "What do you mean?"

"Well," I said, somewhat delicately, "it's just that you have so much here that's already secondhand and not quite working. I just wonder . . ."

"Not working?" she said, putting down her spoon. "Why, everything works, Colie."

I glanced at the TV—JIGGLE TO GET 11—then at the toaster, which was labeled BURNS THINGS FAST! "Yeah," I said, "but don't you ever want something that works perfectly, every time?"

She considered this, looking out at the birdfeeders. "I don't know," she said, as if it had never occurred to her. "I mean, perfect is a lot to expect from something, right? We all have our faults."

"It's not about us," I said gently. "It's a *toaster*."

"It doesn't matter." She sat back in her chair. "If something doesn't work exactly right, or maybe needs some special treatment, you don't just throw it away. Everything can't be fully operational all the time. Sometimes, we need to have the patience to give something the little nudge it needs."

"To jiggle eleven," I said.

"Exactly," she said, pointing at me with her spoon. "See, Colie, it's about understanding. We're all worth *something*."

She went back to her cereal and I glanced around the room, thinking of all her little notes—FAUCET OFF IS HARD LEFT, BIG KNIFE IS SLIGHTLY DULL, WINDOW NEEDS GOOD KNOCK TO OPEN— and her secondhand things, all eventually to be fixed—or at least partially fixed, but used in some way. For Mira, there were no lost causes. Everything, and everyone, had its purpose. The rest of the world, too often, might have missed that

That afternoon I was working with Morgan. She showed up with two dozen deviled eggs. Isabel had warned me about this.

"What?" Morgan said suddenly, putting down the tray of eggs, all white and yellow and perfectly formed, between us. "What is it?"

"Nothing," I said.

"You don't like deviled eggs?"

"I love them."

"Then what is that look for?" Clearly she wasn't her normal cheery self. Still, as she went behind the counter to start the tea machine she picked up my stack of rags and folded them quickly, setting them at a right angle to the silverware station.

"Nothing," I said again, watching her folding, folding, folding, her face irritated. The kitchen door slammed and I looked through the food window to see Norman coming in, a book tucked under his arm. He waved and I was suddenly embarrassed, remembering him shirtless, asleep. I told myself to smile.

"You don't have to eat them," Morgan snapped. When she was angry her face seemed more square. Her hair was newly cut too, straight across her forehead, adding to the effect. "I was trying to be *nice*." She flipped over the napkins.

"I'm sorry," I said. I didn't want Morgan mad at me. "It's just that Isabel told me you'd probably bring in deviled eggs today."

She just looked at me.

"So it was kind of funny."

She wasn't smiling.

"When you did," I finished. "Forget it. I'm sorry."

She sighed and moved the spoons. "Oh, I'm sorry too." She leaned back against the coffee machine. "It's just that Mark left early, and things didn't go the way I wanted them to." She paused. "And I always make deviled eggs when I'm upset. I mean, I guess it *is* kind of funny."

"No," I said solemnly. "It isn't." Norman ambled out of the kitchen, heading toward the storeroom. He came to a sudden, whiplash kind of stop when he saw the eggs.

"Hey!" he said. "Those deviled eggs?"

"Yes," Morgan said quietly.

"With paprika?"

Morgan nodded.

Norman lifted up the edge of the cling wrap, examining the rows and rows of perfect half-eggs underneath. "Wow."

They did smell good.

"Can I, uh, have one?" Norman asked Morgan, who just

covered her eyes with her hand and nodded. He took his time picking one out, selecting it from the top left corner and cradling it in his palm as if it was precious. "Great," he said happily, carefully replacing the cling wrap. "Thanks."

"No problem," Morgan murmured. We watched him walk to the storeroom. He disappeared inside, came out with a bag of hamburger buns, and passed us again, the egg still cupped in his hand.

"Want to savor it," he explained. He went back into the kitchen.

Morgan sighed. "I," she announced, "am so pathetic."

"You are not," I said.

"I am." She went over and straightened the cling wrap, corner to corner. "Do you know how many times I've brought in deviled eggs? This is, like, the only time I haven't been sobbing and that's only 'cause I cried all night. And Norman," she said, her voice rising to a wail, "sweet Norman, always just acts so *surprised* to see the eggs, and pleased, and he never, once, has ever acted like he knew what they meant."

I looked over at the eggs.

"I hate my life!" Morgan cried, breaking down completely, her shoulders shaking. Behind her, the spoons rattled.

"Oh, Morgan," I said helplessly.

She kept crying. In the kitchen, Norman was slowly eating his egg, watching us solemnly.

"It's so awful," she sobbed. "I finally get to see him and he's so distant, he doesn't want to talk about the wedding at all. . . ."

"Oh, Morgan," I said again. What was I supposed to do? In

the movies women hugged and cried and held each other, but that was as foreign to me as another country. I decided to sort the Sweet'n Lows.

She kept crying. I ate an egg. And it probably would have kept up like that forever if Isabel hadn't come through the door.

First she saw the eggs. Then she looked at Morgan.

"Morgan," Isabel said softly, which just set her off again. Isabel came behind the counter and I knew to step out of the way. "Morgan, come on."

Morgan was still crying, that blubbery bouncy kind of sobbing you can't control. "It was bad," she said. Her nose was running. "He didn't even stay for breakfast." The rest was lost in her sobs.

"Oh, honey," Isabel said, stepping forward and putting her arms around Morgan. "What a jerk."

I kept my head down and moved on to stocking straws.

"Don't say you told me so," Morgan said finally into Isabel's shoulder, her voice muffled. "Please don't."

And Isabel shook her head, one hand smoothing Morgan's hair. "I won't."

"Thank you," Morgan sniffled. "I know you're thinking it. . . ."

"I am," Isabel agreed.

"But just don't say it." She pulled back; her eyes were puffy and red, her bangs stuck to her forehead.

"Oh, my God," Isabel said suddenly. "What did you do to your *bangs*, Morgan?"

"I cut them," Morgan said, bursting into another round of tears.

"What did I tell you about messing with your hair when you're upset?"

"I know. I know . . ." Morgan tried to fluff them with her fingers but they were much too short. "I'm having a bad hair day, okay?"

"It's all right," Isabel decided. "We'll fix them later."

"Okay." Morgan sniffled again. "Good."

Isabel looked at the eggs. Then she reached under the cling wrap to slide one out, making a mess in the process. She popped it into her mouth, whole.

I could tell Morgan was itching to fix that plastic but she didn't move.

"Come right home after work," Isabel told her through the mouthful of egg. "We'll do your hair and have a few beers and open the Columbia CD package I got last week."

"A package?" Morgan said, blowing her nose in a napkin. "You didn't tell me we'd gotten another one."

"I," Isabel said, dragging out another egg and putting on her sunglasses, "was saving it for a special occasion. See you later, okay?"

Now, finally, Morgan smiled. "All right. You don't have a date for the fireworks already?"

Isabel chucked that egg in her mouth too, grinning the entire time. Then she shook her head. "Nah. These are *good*," she said. Then she looked at me as she pushed the door open. "You come too, Colie. Okay?"

I was surprised. "Sure," I said.

"Good. It'll be Chick Night." She stepped outside. "Later!"

We watched her walk over to the Rabbit, then make another

123

one of her trademark gravel-scattering exits. As she pulled into traffic, someone speeding by in a pickup truck whooped and beeped at her. And then she was gone.

"Chick Night," Morgan said slowly, walking over and lifting out two eggs. Then she wiped the back of the plastic wrap. "You know, I think that's just what I need right now."

I nodded. She handed me an egg and I took it. We stood there, chewing, until our first customers pulled up.

Chick Night, I thought. Another first for me. I didn't quite know what to expect.

But I would find out soon enough.

We could hear the music from the end of Mira's driveway. I was carrying the tray with the few eggs that were left; I myself had eaten six and was trying not to look at them.

"Ah," Morgan said, as we came closer, the music getting louder and louder. "Disco."

"What?"

She nodded towards the little house. All the lights were on and the door was open. "Disco," she explained, "is great for healing. Not to mention dancing."

At this I froze, my fingers tightening on the egg tray. No one had mentioned anything about dancing.

"I don't dance," I said.

Morgan looked at me. "What?"

"I said I don't dance."

"Everyone dances," Morgan said simply.

"Not me."

She pulled open the door, letting out a burst of music: Sister Sledge, singing "We are Family"; a standard on *Kiki's Disco Years Workout* tape. On it my mother wore a purple leotard and bell-bottoms, doing the Hustle, while three rows of overweight people huffed and puffed behind her.

"You will," she said. And she reached behind her, holding the door open, the music spilling out to greet me.

I didn't dance. And I had my reasons.

As a fat girl, I'd experienced a wide range of humiliations. Add in the fact that I was almost always new, too, and I hit trouble everywhere I went.

Once, in elementary school, I came home after a particularly bad day and gorged myself on Oreos. I sat down with a full package and a half-gallon of milk to drown my sorrows, twisting off the tops and licking out the white insides, one after another.

Thirty minutes later I was in the bathroom, kneeling before the toilet and throwing up black stuff, which swirled away only to be replaced by more black stuff, and more black stuff, for what seemed like an eternity.

I never touched an Oreo again. I honestly cannot even be in the room with one.

I feel the same way about dancing.

It was the Fall Harvest Dance. My first dance. As usual, I was at a new school: Central Middle, in some small suburb of Maryland. My mother was working at a dentist's office; it was the first time in my life I'd had clean, well-inspected teeth.

Maybe this made me feel confident enough to go to the Harvest Dance. Or maybe it was my mother, who never let her extra pounds get in the way of having a little fun. Either way, when I was only two months into a new school, fat with no friends (other fat kids wouldn't hang out with me because I was *new,* part of the complex stratification even among the losers at Central Middle), my mother spent all the grocery money to buy me a new pair of Misses Plus jeans and a cute top.

The top was long-sleeved, with green and pink stripes. I wore my white Keds and a pair of heart-shaped earrings my mom had given me for my birthday. We spent a lot of time selecting this combination, and she even let me wear some of her makeup. She dropped me off on the other side of the football field, the cool thing to do, so I appeared to have just walked out of the woods.

"Have fun," she called after me. I'd gotten the sense, through all the shopping and preparation, that she would have gladly traded places and gone herself. I was more than ready to let her.

The engine of the Volaré rattled as she drove off. "You look great!" she yelled as I stepped through the brush and started across the field. I could already hear the music, could see the lights in the cafeteria, and despite myself I felt a little flutter of excitement.

I paid my three bucks and went inside, passing clumps of kids along the hallway; no one seemed to be dancing yet. The fat girls were all in a far corner. One of them had brought a book and was reading it.

I went to the bathroom and checked my makeup under the glaring fluorescent lights, to see if I looked different. Then I washed my hands twice and went back to the cafeteria.

By then some people were dancing. I went inside and stood against the wall, watching as the most popular kids took the floor, the girls shaking their hips and hair, the boys all doing that same white-guy shuffle with their eyes somewhere else, their faces bored.

It wasn't bad, all of a sudden, being there. Everyone around me was moving to the loud music, even the other fat kids. So I did, too.

No one ever really teaches you how to dance. I was kind of moving back and forth, looking down like everyone else. I couldn't even find myself in the crowd reflected in the cafeteria windows. That was nice.

There was a girl standing next to me with glasses and long hair, and when I looked over she smiled shyly. The music was good and I relaxed, letting myself move a little bit more, copying some of the moves I saw other people making. Maybe this would be different, this school. Maybe I *would* make friends.

I kept dancing, thinking this, and I realized suddenly why people liked to dance; it did feel good. Fun, even.

Then I heard it. Someone laughing. The noise started off quietly, but as the music was dying down, the song changing, it got louder. I looked up, still dancing, to see a boy across the cafeteria with his cheeks puffed out, moving like a hippopotamus, his legs straight and locked, rocking back and forth. Everyone was standing around watching him, giggling. The more they laughed, the more pronounced he became; sticking out his tongue, rolling his eyes back in his head.

It took a few seconds to realize that he was imitating *me*. And by that point everyone was staring.

I stopped moving. The music changed and I glanced around me to see that the girl with the glasses was gone; *everyone* was gone. I'd been all alone, dancing, in my big fat Misses Plus jeans and new shirt.

When this happens in the movies and in after-school specials, the fat, teased kid is always befriended by some nice person who sees her for the wonderful, worthwhile person she really is. But in real life, middle school just isn't like that.

No one followed me as I walked back across the football field and sat beneath a stubby pine tree for two and a half hours, waiting for my mother. I could hear the music from the cafeteria. I could even hear voices through the woods, people sneaking away from the chaperones. When my mother pulled up at ten o'clock I climbed into the car and didn't say a word the whole way home.

I told her later as I sat with her arms around me, crying, my voice hiccuping and ashamed. She just rocked me back and forth, her mouth set in that thin, straight line that meant she was angry. She stroked my hair and told me I was beautiful, but I was old enough by then to know not to believe it anymore.

Two weeks later, she gave up her job at the dentist's and we moved to Massachusetts, where I was the fat new kid all over again. But I never forgot Central Middle or that dance. I never could.

There's something about dancing that's like being stripped

naked; you have to be very self-confident to thrash around in public, deliberately attracting attention. I'd never been that way, even without the weight that once kept me in everyone's eyes. Dancers were the lightest and brightest of butterflies, while girls like me stayed low, bellies scraping the floor, and watched from there.

chapter ten

The first thing I saw when we stepped inside was Isabel, her hair in rollers, crossing the kitchen floor to turn up the CD player. She had on cutoffs and a short white shirt, and her bare feet had cotton balls between each toe. The polish on her toenails was bright red and still looked wet.

"Is this new?" Morgan yelled, as I put the eggs down on the coffee table. Isabel tossed her a CD case before heading back to the kitchen. Morgan turned it over, examining it.

"I love disco," she said.

I nodded. I had my eyes on Mira's house, my excuses ready. I could not stay.

"I bought supplies," Isabel announced, coming back into the

living room with a grocery bag. She started unpacking it, stacking its contents on the table and floor: two six-packs of beer, a six-pack of Diet Coke, *Cosmo,* two bottles of nail polish, a pack of Fudge Stripes, and a plastic container of what looked like cold cream. Then she picked up the bag and shook it, emptying out a handful of Atomic Fireballs, two packs of gum, and some cigarettes; there were a couple of boxes of sparklers, too.

"For you," she said to me, handing over the gum. She gave Morgan the Atomic Fireballs and kept the cigarettes, tucking them in her shorts pocket.

"Isabel," Morgan said disapprovingly. Actually, she yelled. We were all yelling to be heard over the Bee Gees. "You quit, remember?"

"I got you Fudge Stripes," Isabel pointed out. "So hush."

"Fudge Stripes don't kill you," Morgan fussed.

"Morgan." Isabel shook her head. "Let it go, okay? Just for tonight."

"They cause cancer," Morgan said.

"Let it go. . . ." Isabel said, closing her eyes.

"And heart disease."

"Let it go. . . ."

"And emphysema."

"Morgan!" Isabel opened her eyes. *"Let it go!"*

Morgan reached for the Fudge Stripes and sat back on the couch. "Fine," she said, ripping open the package and stuffing one in her mouth in a sloppy, very un-Morgan-like fashion. Then she held them out to me.

"No thanks," I said.

"You never eat anything bad," she said. To Isabel she called out, "Ever noticed that, Is?"

"Noticed what?"

"That Colie eats so healthy, it's disgusting," Morgan said. "I've never even seen her have a french fry."

"And she runs every morning." Isabel came back and plopped down on the floor, reaching for a beer. "I always see her when I get up to pee. She's out there at some ungodly hour."

"Eight o'clock," I said.

"Exactly," Isabel said.

"Well, if Kiki Sparks was *your* mother," Morgan said, her mouth full, "I guess you'd have to be a health freak, right?"

I just nodded. People assumed that, never knowing my mother's favorite food in the Fat Years—and now—was fried pork rinds.

Isabel popped the top off her beer, then handed one to Morgan. She gave me a Diet Coke. "I'd give you a beer," she said, "but . . ."

"But you're underage," Morgan said primly. "And it would be illegal."

Isabel rolled her eyes.

"Well, it would be." Morgan pulled her legs up underneath her. "When I was fifteen I lived off Coke and Reese's cups. I ate Twinkies for breakfast."

"And never gained a pound," Isabel said, reaching for the cold cream. When she opened it, however, it was bright green and oozy, like toxic waste.

"I wanted to gain weight in high school," Morgan said to me. She was alternating between eating deviled eggs and sucking on an Atomic Fireball held between her thumb and forefinger. "I was so skinny you could see my collarbone from a mile off. Disgusting."

"It was not," Isabel said. She smeared a handful of the green stuff across her face, covering her cheeks and forehead.

"Plus I was ten feet taller than any of the boys," Morgan went on. "And since my mom never wanted to buy me any new clothes and I kept growing, all my skirts and pants were too short. My nickname was Highwater."

"Do we *have* to talk about high school?" Isabel said. Now her entire face was green, except for a tiny bit of white around her eyes and mouth. She handed the container to Morgan.

"You're right." Morgan spit out the Fireball and sat cross-legged, scooping out a green handful. "I'm depressed enough already."

"Wait, wait," Isabel said. "I don't want to talk about Mark, either."

But Morgan was already going. "The thing is," she began, a glob of green in one hand, "it was stupid for me to get so upset, anyway. I mean, it's not his fault his schedule is so crazy right now. He might be getting moved up to Triple A next year, the team is doing really well . . ."

"Whatever," Isabel said. The green stuff on her face, which I had finally figured out was some kind of beauty mask, was hardening and forming tiny cracks whenever she spoke.

". . . and the last thing he needs when he finally gets a chance

133

to see me is to be bombarded with details about the wedding and our future. It's no wonder he gets so irritated when I bug him about it."

"Morgan," Isabel said. Her voice sounded strange; she was trying not to move her mouth. "Don't forget how upset you were this morning."

"I haven't," Morgan said, glancing at her ring. She spread the mask across her face, carefully, using her fingertips.

Isabel leaned back, pulling the cigarettes out of her pocket. "Because that's what you always do, you know. You get all upset and then just forget it away."

"You can't smoke in here," Morgan snapped. Then she got up and went to the kitchen, turning the music up even louder.

"I wasn't going to," Isabel shouted after her. Then she nodded toward the face stuff. "Go ahead," she said. "It's your turn."

I picked it up, peering down into the green contents.

"Don't tell me you've never done this before," she said.

"Well," I said.

"Oh, God." She crouched down in front of me. "Give it to me."

Morgan was still in the kitchen, washing her hands. I could see her green face reflected in the window over the sink.

Isabel scooped out a handful of mask and leaned close to me, spreading big gobs of it across my skin. It was cool and smelled like leaves.

"All natural," she explained, her finger brushing my lip ring as some slipped into my mouth. It tasted terrible. "Deep-cleans your pores and tightens the skin. What kind of person has never done a beauty mask before? When I was fifteen I was obsessed with this stuff."

"Colie's not like we were," Morgan said, coming back to sit beside me. She'd pulled her hair back in a clip on top of her head and looked like a big asparagus. "She doesn't sit home and read *Seventeen* every Saturday night. She has a *life.*"

Isabel kept spreading the mask. I waited for her to say something about Caroline Dawes and what she'd heard, but she didn't. Instead, she just sat back and looked at my face, studying her work. "Oh, right," she said. "A life."

Morgan reached over and picked up the phone. "Hello?" she said.

I was confused for a second until I realized it must have rung. Morgan, obviously, had doglike super hearing.

"Turn that down," she hissed, pointing at the CD player.

"Who is it?" Isabel said, getting up.

"Just turn it down."

"Oh," Isabel said, slowing down considerably. "It's Mark." She cocked her head to the side, hard, to punctuate the name.

"Turn it *down,* Is."

Isabel turned it down and the noise was sucked out, gone, just like that. Then she came back over, plopped down on the floor, and opened another beer.

"I wasn't mad," Morgan was saying, her mask cracking as she did so. She wrapped the phone cord around her fingers. "I just really wanted to have a chance to talk about our future. . . ."

"Oh, God," Isabel said loudly, and Morgan turned her back.

"I know. I know how busy you are." Morgan examined her nails, one by one. "I just always forget how little time you have to spend with me."

Isabel made a gagging noise. Morgan stood, picked up the phone, and started dragging it toward the bedroom, still talking.

"Ask him why he'll never give you a number where you can reach him," Isabel called out as the cord slid along the floor. "Ask him why he only calls you once a *week*."

Morgan waved her off angrily, trying to get the door shut.

"And ask him about that girl in Wilson, Morgan. Get a spine and ask him for *once* about that."

The door slammed. Isabel threw up her hands.

"That girl," she said, in the same loud voice, "wants to be hurt. And I am *so sick* of standing by and watching her do it." Her green mask was splitting open across her cheeks. "Let me tell you something about men, Colie."

I waited. My skin felt strange, tight, and I was concentrating on not moving any part of my face.

"Men," Isabel said, after pausing to suck down some beer, "are wired, by nature, to take everything they can from you. It is their basic instinct to screw you over."

"Really."

"Yes," she said solidly. Then she leaned closer. "If you think that girl from the restaurant yesterday can hurt you, you just wait. All the bitchy girls in the world are just a training ground for what men can do to you."

The bedroom door opened and Morgan stood there, phone under her arm. Even with her green face I could tell she was mad.

"What is your *problem?*" she snapped, dropping the phone onto the couch. "He heard what you were saying, Isabel. He heard you."

"Good."

"I don't understand," Morgan huffed, "why you have to bad-mouth him to anyone who will listen."

"I'm not the one coming to work and sobbing over him, Morgan," Isabel shot back. "I'm not the one bringing in deviled eggs."

"This isn't about deviled eggs," Morgan said.

"No, it isn't." Isabel picked up her pack of cigarettes, turning it over and over in her hand. "This is about how Mark does not respect you. About how he *uses* you."

"Shut up," Morgan said in a tired voice, walking into the kitchen.

"Why doesn't he ever ask you to come to the games? And why can you never get a number or place where he's at or going to be since you surprised him in Wilson?"

"He's never sure where exactly he'll—"

"Bullshit!" Isabel yelled. "You can go down to the drugstore and buy a poster for ninety-nine cents with their entire sched-ule on it. They're a baseball team, Morgan. They have a *season*. They don't just travel around playing random teams when they feel like it."

Morgan put her hands on her hips. "It's more complicated than that. You don't know—"

"I know this," Isabel said, standing up. "I know he comes into town, sleeps with you, and books out of here the next day before breakfast. I know when you went to surprise him on your anniversary you found that stripper in his hotel room." She was ticking things off on her fingers, one by one. "And," she went on, "I know that since he gave you that 'ring'"—as she said it she made quote marks with her fingers—"he has not said one word about your wedding or your future. *Not one word.*"

Morgan absorbed this, blinking. She'd put one hand over her ring, protectively, when Isabel mentioned it.

My face was so tight my eyes were starting to hurt. But getting up to wash the mask off meant stepping between them, and I wasn't about to do that.

"Can't you see, Morgan?" Isabel lowered her voice and took a few steps closer; with their green faces, they looked like aliens meeting on a foreign planet. "There's something wrong here."

Morgan blinked again. I wondered if she was going to cry.

Then she straightened up to her full height and took a deep breath. *"Jealous!"* she shouted, pointing a long bony finger at Isabel, who just rolled her eyes. "You always have been! Since the very beginning!"

"Oh, please," Isabel said indignantly.

"You are," Morgan said, turned on her heel, and went down the hallway to the bathroom. "Because *you* weren't his type."

"Oh, that's right, Morgan," Isabel yelled, following her even as the bathroom door slammed shut. "I want to be the one engaged to a baseball player who's already balding, cheats on me with other women, can never give me a straight answer about the rest of our lives, and couldn't get over the Mendoza Line if his life depended on it!"

There was a silence. Then Morgan opened the door.

"His batting average," she said coolly, "has greatly improved this season."

"I don't give a shit!" Isabel screamed.

The door slammed shut again.

"Mendoza Line?" I said.

Isabel stomped back to the living room, cranking up the music. "It's a baseball thing. It means he sucks."

"He does not!" Morgan yelled from the bathroom. "He doesn't even lead the team in errors anymore!"

Isabel grabbed her cigarettes and kicked open the screen door. I watched her strike a match, its orange glow lighting up her face, before she moved down the porch, out of sight.

The disco was still blasting. My face felt like it had been dipped and set in concrete. From the kitchen window I could see Mira's house, quiet and peaceful. I wondered if she knew that she didn't really need wrestling at all. Morgan and Isabel were like Triple Threat and Saturday Cage Fights rolled into one.

I turned down the music, then walked down the hallway and knocked on the bathroom door.

"What?" Morgan said.

"I really need to wash my face," I said.

"Oh." I heard her get up. "Okay."

She unlocked the door and I pushed it open, sliding inside. She was sitting on the edge of the tub, her mask streaked and muddy from crying. I pretended not to notice.

I went to the sink and ran the water until it was warm, then carefully washed off the mask, watching the green run down the drain. Morgan handed me a towel.

"Colie," she said as I patted myself dry, noticing that my skin did actually feel very nice, "do you have a best friend?"

I looked down at the towel, folding it carefully. It was, after all, Morgan's. "I don't have any friends," I said.

"Oh, that's not true," she said in the quick, knee-jerk way of guidance counselors and teachers.

"Yeah," I said. "It is." I handed her the towel.

There was an awkward silence, made even more noticeable because the bathroom was so small. I had nothing to look at but my hands, Morgan, or my own face in the mirror.

"Well," she said, and I could tell she was uncomfortable now, sorry she'd even brought it up, "sometimes they're more trouble than they're worth."

I didn't know what to say to that. Trouble or not, at least she wasn't alone.

"I love Mark so much," she blurted out. "And Isabel is just wrong about him. I would know if he wasn't the one. I mean, I'd have to *know*, right?"

"She's just worried about you," I said. "She doesn't want you to get hurt." I could understand this, because it was not unlike the way my mother had always taken care of me.

"She needs to butt out," Morgan sniffled. "This is my life. She's my best friend but this is *my life*."

There was a silence. Morgan was still sniffling, dabbing at her face with the towel, which was now splotched with green. This was my first true confessions session in a bathroom, a Girl Moment, plain and simple. I had to say *something*.

"When I first met you, you said Isabel wasn't so bad," I told her. She looked up, her clear skin showing through in patches. "You just said she could be a real bitch sometimes. And that she was friendship-impaired."

"Oh," she said. "I did?"

"Yeah."

"Well, she is impaired," she admitted. "She didn't know how to be friends because she'd never had one. Until me."

I could feel my own earlier admission hanging in the air like smoke between us And now I might have told Morgan about my fat Harvest Dance, and all the schools I'd suffered through and left behind. But, again, there was something that stopped me, that prevented me from opening myself like a book to the spine, leaving the pages exposed.

"I'm just saying," I told her, "that maybe you should remember that about her when you guys fight like this."

She nodded. "I do," she said softly. "I can't ever forget it. It's, like, part of who she is, you know?"

"I know." And I did.

Outside in the living room, the music suddenly cut off. There were a few minutes of silence, broken only by the sound of Isabel going through the stacks of CDs. Then a click as she shut the top of the player and another as she hit the button.

The music started.

"At first I was afraid, I was petrified . . ."

Morgan went to the sink. She splashed at her face, again and again, until the water didn't run green anymore. Then she lifted her head and smiled at her reflection, at the bits of green speckled here and there along her hairline. "She's so crazy," she said to me softly. But she was smiling.

"Kept thinking I could never live without you by my side. . . ."

And outside the door, suddenly, I heard Isabel singing along. *"But then I spent so many nights thinking how you did me wrong!"*

"And I grew strong!" Morgan yelled back. *"And I learned how to get along!"*

The door flew open and there was Isabel, arms over her head, hips shaking, eyes closed as she channeled some long-ago disco queen. Her face was green, her curlers bobbing madly.

"And so you're back from outer space," she sang, off-key.

"I just walked in to find you here with that sad look upon your face. . . ." Morgan moved forward, past me, snapping her fingers over her head while Isabel turned and started shimmying down the hallway. Morgan followed, skipping from side to side, doing some sort of strange booty-slap.

It was like the first night I'd seen them, and I wished I was back on Mira's roof, watching from a safe distance.

I walked behind them, keeping my eyes on the door. It was like being caught in some weird tribal ritual, firewalking or glass swallowing, and not knowing the correct way to carefully extract yourself. I dodged when they started doing the bump, Isabel's energetic hip swings knocking Morgan halfway across the room, and put my hand on the screen door. They had completely forgotten me.

"Colie!"

Or maybe not.

I turned back, pushing the door open as I did so. "Yeah?"

"Come on!" Morgan was waving me over as she shook her hips. The music was still cranking and the song, the stupid song, seemed to be endless.

"I have to—"

But now she was coming over, still dancing, and reached out to grab my hand. "Come *on*," she said, and gave me a good yank, pulling me back toward them.

"I told you," I yelled back at her, over the music, "I don't dance."

"We'll show you," she said, misunderstanding me. The song was ending now, fading out note by note.

"No," I said, loudly, pulling my arm back. She looked surprised, then hurt, and it was suddenly very quiet, with just the last bits of my loud objection settling around us.

"What is your problem?" Isabel said.

"I don't dance." I folded my arms across my chest, taking all of myself back. "I told you that." And I didn't care if they laughed at me, or hated me. I didn't care what they would say when I was gone.

They exchanged looks. Isabel shrugged. "Whatever," she said. Then she reached up and undid one of her curlers, a perfect blonde corkscrew falling down over her eyes. "We need to get ready, anyway."

"Yeah," Morgan agreed, but she looked more hesitant, still watching my face. "We do."

"Ready?" I said.

"To go out," Isabel said over her shoulder. "You really haven't done a Chick Night, have you?"

"No," I said.

"Well, hurry up," Morgan scolded me. "And shut that door. We have work to do."

chapter eleven

"You can't have a good Chick Night," Morgan said, leaning in to the mirror to curl her eyelashes, "without at least one cat-fight."

"And somebody has to cry, at least once," Isabel said. "With us, it's usually Morgan."

"Is not," Morgan said, fluffing her bangs, now somewhat fixed.

Isabel caught my eye in the mirror and nodded.

I was sitting on the bed as they stood in front of Isabel's tiny vanity, adding on and tweezing away, emphasizing and conceal-ing with the spread of makeup before them. The entire room smelled of perfume and smoke, the latter from the curling iron that Isabel had accidentally set on a stack of magazines. The fire had been small but dramatic, burning Cindy Crawford's lovely face to a crisp.

The closest I'd come to this was watching my mother get ready for dates, something I'd been doing for as long as I could remember. Even in the Fat Years, my mother made time for a social life. It was my job to sit on the bed and hold the box of Kleenex, handing them over as needed to rub in blush or blot lipstick. It was also my job to answer the door, lead her date to the one good chair that always traveled with us—a recliner we'd bought off the side of the road in Memphis for fifty bucks—and make small talk until my mother made her entrance, smelling of whatever perfume insert had been in *Cosmo* that month.

This was different. This time, I was the one who was going.

"Sit up straight," Isabel scolded after I'd been sat, on orders, in the chair facing the mirror. "Slouching is the first dead give-away of low self-esteem."

I sat up.

She pulled back my hair with a headband, then scrutinized my face. "Morgan."

"Yes?"

"Hand me that Revlon Sand Beige makeup. And a sponge. And the tweezers." She held her hand out flat, like a surgeon waiting for a scalpel.

"The tweezers?" I said as Morgan slapped them efficiently into her palm.

"Good eyebrows take maintenance," she said, leaning forward with her eyes narrowed. "Deal with it."

She plucked. I sat there, staring again at all the beautiful girls while she worked her magic. She spread makeup over my face, blending and dabbing until all of its normal bumps and ridges were smoothed away. She curled my eyelashes as I squirmed, her hand fixed hard on my shoulder. She lined my eyes with black kohl, smudging it with her thumb, then brushed blush on my cheeks and added mascara, drawing my lashes out farther and farther. Then she pulled my hair back, letting a few strands wind down, just like hers. And all the while I studied those perfect faces, one after another, until I came back to my own.

And I saw a girl. Not a fat girl, or a loser, or even a golf course slut.

A pretty girl. Something I had never been before.

"Sit up straight," Isabel said again, poking me in the spine with the hairbrush. "And put your shoulders back."

I did.

"Now smile."

I smiled. In the mirror, over my head, Isabel frowned.

"Do me a favor," she said, leaning in so her face was right beside mine. "Can you take that thing out?"

She was pointing at my lip ring, and I instantly ran my tongue across it. It was my touchstone, after all. I needed it. "Um," I said. "I don't know."

"Just for one night," she said. "Humor me."

And I looked back at myself in the mirror, at all those faces, and then glanced at Isabel's cousin. She stared back through her thick glasses, her face plump and wide.

"Okay," I said. "But just for one night."

"One night," she agreed, as I reached up to take it out, the last remaining part of what I once was. "One night."

Chase Mercer had been new to the neighborhood, just like me. His dad did something in software and drove two Porsches, a blue and a red. He didn't fit in much at first either, since he had a sister in a wheelchair; she had something wrong with her legs, and a nurse wheeled her up and down the street every day. Whenever she saw me, she waved. She waved at everyone.

I met Chase at a neighborhood pool party at the country club. We were both with our parents. The adults were clumped around the bar, my mother working the crowd, and all the kids had disappeared to do whatever kids did in Conroy Plantations, so Chase and I started walking across the golf course. It was late summer and all the stars were out. We were just talking. Nothing else.

He was from Columbus, with thick blond hair that stuck up in the back. He liked sports and Super Nintendo, and when he was six he'd had pneumonia so bad he'd almost died. His mother sold real estate and was never home, and his sister had been sick since she was born and her name was Andrea. He missed his old friends and his old school, and all the kids he'd met in Conroy Plantations were rich and obnoxious and cared too much about clothes.

I told Chase Mercer about my mother suddenly becoming famous. About my father, whom I'd never seen aside from a picture of him and my mother standing by the Alamo, in Texas. About how all the girls in Conroy Plantations made fun of me because I'd been fat and were only nice to me when their mothers made them.

I told Chase Mercer a lot of things.

We ended up sitting on the grass at the eighteenth hole, both of us staring up at the stars. Chase knew almost all the constellations—he'd had a telescope in Columbus—and he was picking them out, one finger pointing while I followed it with my eyes. He had just spotted Cassiopeia when I heard the voices.

"Yoo-hoo!" Then a light flickered across my face, a flashlight beam darting from me to Chase and back again. "Oh, my God," someone shrieked. There was an explosion of giggling. "Chase, you *dog,* you," someone else yelled out.

"Shut up," Chase said. He stood up and brushed himself off, raising one hand to shield his eyes from the light.

"I always knew she was a slut," I heard a girl say, and even without looking I knew it had to be Caroline Dawes, who was skinny and tan, with straight black hair she spent a lot of time swinging around. Her mother had made her invite me over just after I moved in, and we'd spent a long, painful afternoon in her room, where, as I watched, she lay on the bed talking on the phone. We'd already been in gym class together for almost two years, and she'd tortured me with every fat name in the book until I'd lost the weight. Now, with my awful luck, we were neighbors, and she had something new to hold against me.

"Let's go," someone said, and the light flicked across us once more, landing square on my face. It hurt my eyes. "Oh, gross," another voice said. "Chase, you must have been *desperate,* man."

I turned to look at Chase but he was walking away, quickly, his head down. "Chase," I called out.

"Oh, *Chase,*" someone echoed in a high falsetto. More laughing. But they were leaving now, their voices growing fainter, the light skipping across the trees and grass, brightening their path.

"Wait," I said, but I could hardly see him now. The voices trailed off and I was left there alone, under all those stars.

By the next morning when I went to the pool, I had a new nickname: Hole in One. And when I saw Chase Mercer at the snack bar, he wouldn't even look at me. He walked right over to where Caroline Dawes and all her friends were sitting, greasing themselves up with baby oil and drinking Diet Coke, and took his place with them.

Chase Mercer got off easy.

A week later, just before school started, I went downtown to a tattoo place and had my lip pierced. I don't know why I did it; it just felt right. I figured I had nothing to lose.

It was the same reason I cut my hair with nail scissors and dyed it bright red. The same reason I took up with Ben Lucas, who was nasty and dirty and just wanted to get into my pants, and I almost let him. The same reason I lost myself in music that screamed and thundered and hated as much as I wanted to.

And I sat in my new bedroom in my new house with my new pool and new clothes and felt miserable, angry with every inch of who I was. At school I was like a time bomb, ready to explode; I pulled my long coat around me for protection so that nothing could get through.

It worked, as well as it could.

At school the guidance counselor, Ms. Young, would pat me on the shoulder and tell me all I needed was a little self-esteem. "And a role model," she'd go on cheerfully. "Someone you admire who is strong and fearless, who you can model yourself after."

I didn't have anyone but my mother. And I knew she wasn't strong all the time. She'd been fat in school, too.

"Oh, honey," my mother would say, stroking my hair. "These are the worst years. I promise you." But this time, she couldn't quit her job and take me someplace else. We were here to stay.

The worst years, I'd repeat to myself, thinking of Caroline Dawes and Chase Mercer and Hole in One and the music that almost, but never quite, pounded them all away. And then I'd run my tongue across my lip and hope that she was right.

Morgan drove. Isabel rode shotgun, and I sat in the back, with all the CDs and magazines and a hairbrush that bounced across my lap each time we took a turn. The radio was blasting, but Morgan and Isabel talked the whole time. I couldn't hear a word they said; instead I caught bits and pieces of their laughing faces in the light from oncoming cars, Morgan rolling her eyes, Isabel with her feet balanced on the dashboard, singing along with the radio.

I kept trying to glimpse my own reflection each time a car lit up the rearview mirror; I was sure I'd find the old me staring back, my hair ragged and black, my lip ring glinting. Instead, I saw that same pretty girl Isabel had created. And I was surprised every time, sure she wasn't real.

It seemed there *was* some social life in Colby and we found it at the public beach. The Colby fireworks were the event of the summer. We took our place, parking at the end of a long row of cars by some dunes.

Morgan opened her door and the dome light came on. Isabel pulled down the visor and looked in her mirror. "Nose check," she said.

Morgan peered in the rearview, turning up her head and checking her nostrils. "Okay here."

"Here too."

"How's my lipstick?" Morgan asked.

Isabel glanced at her. "Good. Mine?"

"Good."

If this was what girls did, I wasn't quite sure I really wanted to know about it.

Isabel turned around. "Ready?" she asked me.

It's easier to be ready when you don't know what for. "Sure," I said.

"Okay then. Let's go."

She grabbed one of her six-packs and got out, kicking the door shut; Morgan held the seat for me. She pulled a blanket from the back, folding it in her arms, and carefully locked the door behind us. By that time, Isabel was already halfway across the dunes.

"What is taking you guys so long?" she yelled. "Morgan, don't lock the damn car."

"It's my car," Morgan said, but not loud enough to be heard. She didn't notice that Isabel's window was down.

We walked across the dunes, following Isabel, who, as usual, didn't wait. As my eyes adjusted I could make out groups sitting along the beach. I watched as Isabel smiled at certain people, a beer now dangling from one hand, the rest of the six-pack tucked under her arm. When we passed them, I saw each time that they were couples: a smiling guy and a girl who scowled at Isabel as she walked on.

Isabel kept on going, then finally dropped the six-pack on a small patch of empty sand. I could see bonfires all up and down the beach.

"Here we are," she announced, sitting down as Morgan spread out the blanket. "Big social night in Colby."

"Huge," Morgan agreed, reaching over and helping herself to a beer. She glanced over my head, squinting, and said, "Hey, isn't that Norman?"

It was. He was with a group of people sitting around a bonfire. Of course, he was wearing sunglasses: red ones with oval lenses. When he saw us he smiled and waved.

"Okay," Morgan said in a low voice. "Incoming."

"What?" I said

"Shhh."

Isabel took another sip of beer and threw her shoulders back. Then she acted surprised to see the guy with dark hair and a green plaid shirt who was suddenly standing on our blanket

"Hey," he said to her, taking what even I could tell was a quick mandatory glance over at me and Morgan. He had very white teeth. "Wanna sell me a beer?"

Isabel looked at her supply, then back at him. "I don't know," she said slowly.

"I promise I'll drink it here," he said, leaning down a little closer.

"Gag," Morgan whispered to me. "Old line."

"I don't care where you drink it," Isabel said simply. "I just don't know if I want to give one up."

"I'm worth it," the guy said.

That made her smile. "Score," Morgan whispered.

"We'll see," she said. And he sat down.

"I'm Frank," he said.

"Isabel," she replied. She still hadn't give him a beer. "That's Morgan, and that's Colie."

"Hi," he said to us. But he only took his eyes off Isabel for a second.

Morgan sighed, taking another prim sip of beer. Then she looked up at the dark sky and said, "Fireworks should begin soon."

"Hey, Colie," Isabel called out. "Come here."

I got up and went over. She cupped her hand around my ear and said, "Go back to the car and get my other six-pack, will you? It's under the front seat."

There was a crackling overhead, and everyone looked up. It was starting.

"Okay," I said, standing up straight again. But she grabbed my shirttail and pulled me back down.

"Walk with your head up high," she said quietly, firmly. "Shoulders back. Don't smile. And don't look at anyone. You're gorgeous tonight, Colie. Show yourself off a little. Okay?"

"Whispering's impolite," Morgan said from the other side of the blanket.

"She's going back to the car for me."

As I walked, I could feel people looking at me. I didn't have my lip ring or my long coat. I didn't have my fat or even my tray and apron to hide behind. I had to fight to keep my head up, to not slouch, to shut out everyone around me.

Keep your head up. Shoulders back. Don't smile.

I could hear myself breathing. I'd always stayed on the perimeter of crowds. But now, as I walked, I slowly gained confidence. There was nothing about me so grotesque or strange that it attracted attention. I blended in.

You're gorgeous tonight, Colie. Show yourself off a little.

Could it have been this easy all along? Did I just need to lose weight, enlist the help of Revlon, Miss Clairol, and a wicked set of tweezers, and change my life forever?

I couldn't believe it. If only I'd known, somehow, and found out sooner—

Suddenly someone bumped into me, hard, one of those jarring hits that you feel all the way down to your toes.

I stumbled, catching myself just before I fell completely. And I felt that familiar shame wash over me. I was a big, fat, ugly loser. I didn't deserve to be pretty. Not even for a second.

"Oh, man," I heard someone say. And then there was a hand on my arm. "Are you okay? Man."

I looked up. There was a boy standing beside me—touching me—a cute boy with brown hair and brown eyes, in a white T-shirt and shorts. He had a drink in his hand, now spilled, and he looked worried.

"I'm okay," I said. And I quickly straightened up.

"I'm sorry," he said, and he smiled. "I'm, like, so clumsy."

"It's okay."

He stood there, still smiling at me. *This* was new.

"Oh," he said. "I'm Josh."

"I'm Colie."

"Hi, Colie." Overhead, there was the first official bang, and a shower of red sparks falling. Everyone cheered. "You here with your family?"

"No, just some friends," I said, nodding back toward Morgan and Isabel. I wondered if they were watching.

"Josh!" someone yelled from behind him. "Come on!"

He glanced back, then looked at me again. "I have to go," he said. "But, uh, maybe I'll catch up with you later?"

"Sure," I said.

"Okay," he said. "Cool. And look, I'm sorry. Again."

"No problem."

"Josh!" Someone was getting impatient.

"See ya," he said, and he reached out—quickly—and squeezed my arm. Then he turned and jogged off, glancing back to smile at me.

I waited until he was lost in the crowd before looking back toward our blanket. Morgan watched the sky, but Isabel had her eyes on me. I smiled. She just held up her beer, pointing at it.

Back to business.

I went to the car and got the six-pack. By then the fireworks were in full swing, popping and crackling overhead. The crowd oohed and ahhed. I picked my way through the blankets, trying to spot Morgan and Isabel.

"Colie," someone said, and I felt a tap on my leg. It was Norman.

"Hey," I said.

"Sit down," he said, smoothing some sand for me with the flat of his hand.

"I'm with Morgan and Isabel," I said, and as I scanned the crowd in front of me I found them again. Frank had his head ducked down, talking earnestly to Isabel, who was half listening and half watching the fireworks. Morgan looked bored.

"Oh," he said, as there was another boom and shower of sparks overhead. "Okay. Sure."

We both looked up, watching them fall. Norman said, "You know, it's weird, but every time I see you, you look different, Colie."

I glanced down at him. Two boys in one night being nice to me. I could get used to this. "Thanks," I said. "It's Isabel. I'm kind of a work in progress."

"You look great," he said again. "You know, I've been meaning to ask you . . ."

Just then I saw Josh, walking with a group of guys. He was laughing, and then, somehow, he saw me. And smiled.

". . . how you'd feel about sitting for a portrait. You know, for my series." Norman was still talking. I could hear him, but I was still watching Josh, who was watching me. "I've got to finish it in the next couple of weeks, and I thought . . ."

"That would be great," I said. Josh waved. I waved back.

"You think?" Norman said. "'Cause I really didn't know how you'd feel about it."

"Great," I said again. Josh and his friends stopped by a bonfire further down the beach. He turned back and gestured for me to come over.

"Okay, great," Norman said. "When can you start? I mean, you could come down later tonight or something. I make great hot chocolate. I have this hot plate. It's world-known."

"Yeah, okay," I said, hardly listening; I just knew he was saying something about chocolate. "I should go."

"Great!" There was another pop and crackle overhead. "I'll be up late, so just come whenever."

"Right. I'll see you later, Norman."

I picked my way back to our blanket, as the fireworks got louder and louder.

"Finally," Isabel said when she saw me. "What took you so long?"

"Nothing." I dropped the six-pack next to her and sat down beside Morgan, who was peeling the label off her beer and yawning. Then I turned and looked back. Josh was still watching me.

"Come on," he mouthed, waving. His friends, some of them with girls now, were all grouped around the fire, smoking cigarettes and laughing.

"What is that look on your face?" Morgan said. "Colie?"

I stood up. I was ready to walk over there, to a cute boy with brown eyes who I'd met under the falling sparks of an Independence Day.

"Come on," Josh said.

This was where it started.

"I'm going to go," I said out loud, and Morgan looked up at me. "I—"

Then I saw her. Caroline Dawes. She stepped out from behind one of Josh's friends, turning her head to look in my direction. And she saw me, her nose instantly wrinkling in distaste, as if she'd smelled something bad.

"Come on," Josh said again, waving me over, insistent now. There was another burst of color and light over my head.

But I froze, my eyes on Caroline, who looked from me to Josh and then to me again. She reached out and tapped him on the shoulder. He turned around. And then she said something.

"Colie?" Morgan said. "What is it?"

It was happening again. No matter what I did, or how the world changed for me, all it took was Caroline Dawes to ruin everything.

Then I heard Isabel.

"Colie," she said, and her voice was very clear through the noise swirling around us. "Go."

"I can't," I said. I knew then that she had seen Josh bump into me and everything else. And she'd recognized Caroline Dawes when she stepped out from beside that fire and showed herself.

"Go," she said again. And she nodded her head towards Josh. "Now. Do it."

"What is going on?" Morgan said. "What are you guys talking about?"

But Isabel just watched me. And I remembered all the times I'd let Caroline Dawes ruin my life. That first dance, and the boy who'd imitated me. And, finally, I thought of my mother,

159

standing before thousands of caterpillars, believing them into butterflies.

"Go," Isabel said again. I could tell by her voice, by the way she looked at me, that she knew I would.

And somehow, I stood up and I went.

It was like I was dreaming as I walked across the sand, past all of the upturned faces, the sky coloring over them.

Josh was waiting for me by the bonfire. Caroline stood off to one side, her arms crossed over her chest. She was laughing.

The fireworks were reaching their peak now. I could hear "The Star-Spangled Banner," its tinkly notes rising and falling with each boom and crash. In the midst of all of the noise and color, I told myself I had to look at Caroline Dawes. Every other time she'd been mean I'd let her words just sink down over me, like a blanket shaken out by the corners. But this was going to be different. Whatever she said to me, I would take head-on.

I remembered Isabel, the day she'd taken me home and begun to set me straight. And I saw her tap her temple with one finger, her face close to mine, saying: *Believe in yourself up here and it will make you stronger than you could ever imagine.*

And my mother's words: *Being self-confident doesn't necessarily start inside. It starts with the rest of the world, and leads back to you.*

Then, with one huge, spectacular explosion, the fireworks were over. And the crowd cheered and clapped, whistling with appreciation.

I stood up straight, put my shoulders back, and looked at Caroline Dawes.

This seemed to throw her. I looked at her hard, focusing on the white and brown of her eyes. They were just normal, nothing more. She didn't look away, but I didn't expect her to. We stared at each other for what seemed like a very long time as everyone started to pack up and walk to their cars. The show was over.

"Hey," I heard Josh say. He took a few steps toward me. "What took you so long?"

"I can't believe you," Caroline said to me in her snarky voice. She was really too pretty a girl to be so ugly. "You don't belong here."

I didn't say anything. I didn't have to. Just being there was enough, for now.

"She's a slut," she told Josh, and I watched how her mouth twisted with the words. "Everyone knows it at home."

And Josh glanced at her, then at me. I suddenly realized I didn't care whether he believed her or not. I didn't care what happened next. I had faced the enemy. The rest of the battle was just details.

"You're pathetic," she said to me, and started to turn away.

"And you're such a bitch," I said back. And I laughed, surprised at how my voice sounded, strong and steady. "I feel sorry for you, Caroline."

"I hate you," she snapped.

"You should get over that," I told her. And I imagined Isabel, eyes closed, saying these same words. "It's unhealthy. Just let it go."

Her mouth fell open.

I felt someone beside me. "Come on," Isabel said, closing her fingers over mine. "We're going." Caroline looked at her, the way pretty girls do at girls who are much prettier.

"Okay," I said, and I smiled at her. We started to walk off but Josh ran after us.

"Colie," he said, and beyond him I could see Caroline still watching, her friends all around her. She was talking angrily, the words spewing out. I didn't have to wonder what she was saying about me. I'd heard it all before.

"Yeah?"

"I, um, I'm sorry about my cousin," he said. "We're leaving tomorrow night, but maybe I can call you or something?"

Beside me, Isabel shuffled her feet in the sand. I could see Morgan crossing the dunes, the blanket folded neatly in her arms.

"I work at the Last Chance," I told him, as Isabel tugged me away. "You can find me there."

"I," Morgan said as we bumped down the dirt road toward home, "have no idea what happened tonight."

"I'll tell you everything later," Isabel said to her, patting her knee. "But it was very, very cool."

When we pulled into the driveway, the headlights lit up the front porch, where a man was sitting on the steps. He stood up and squinted at us.

"Oh," Morgan said, one hand flying up to her mouth.

"Oh," Isabel groaned. "Great."

"Mark!" Morgan shrieked, hardly even pausing to stop the car before she got out and ran across the grass, up the steps and into his arms. We were rolling toward the beach until Isabel reached down and yanked up the e-brake. "I thought you were back in Durham tonight."

"Plans changed," he said. "I wanted to surprise you."

We watched from the car as they kissed, a movie-style kiss that lasted for a long time.

"Great," Isabel grumbled. "*Now* where am I supposed to go?"

"Come over to Mira's."

"Nah. I think I'll just take Frank up on that clambake on the sound side. I can walk from here." She got out of the car and held the seat for me, then reached down and salvaged the last of her beers, tucking one in each pocket of her shorts.

"Hey, Isabel," Mark called to her through the dark.

"What's up, Mark," she replied tonelessly.

"I want you to meet Colie," Morgan said, taking him by the hand, leading him down the steps and over to me. As he got closer, I saw he looked just like his picture. Not everyone does. He was tall and tan, very athletic, with short black hair and white teeth that seemed to glow in the dark. "Colie, this is Mark. Mark, this is Colie."

"Hi," he said. "Morgan's told me a lot about you."

"I'm going," Isabel announced. She was already halfway down the driveway.

"Where?" Morgan called after her, but Isabel didn't answer.

"Some clambake," I explained. "With that guy she met at the fireworks."

"So that's where you were," Mark said, slipping his arm around Morgan's waist. She had the goofiest smile on her face. "I missed everything."

"No you didn't," she said suddenly. She reached into her back pocket and pulled out a box, then opened it and shook something out into her hand. "Got a match?"

Mark handed her a lighter and she flicked it, then held the long object toward the flame, stepping back as it erupted into a shower of sparks between us.

"The sparklers," I said. I'd forgotten all about them.

"Happy Fourth of July," she said to Mark, and he kissed her.

I started toward Mira's, wanting some time alone to savor everything that had happened, from the Chick Night to my triumph over Caroline Dawes.

"Colie, stay and light these with us," Morgan called after me.

"I should go," I said.

"Okay. But here. Catch."

And she threw the sparklers at me, the box turning end over end in the air before I caught it in both hands. "Happy Fourth of July," I said, but they didn't hear me.

I closed the door carefully, then slid my hand into my pocket and retrieved my lip ring, carefully securing it back in its proper place. I took off my shoes and tiptoed down the hallway; I didn't know how late it was, but I didn't want to wake Mira.

I shouldn't have worried. Before I'd taken two steps, I heard her voice.

"Hey there." She was sitting in her chair, a disassembled telephone in her lap. I recognized it: it was the one from the upstairs hallway, which had a VERY QUIET RING. "How were the fireworks?"

"Good," I said. I walked over and sat down beside her. The entire house was dark, except for the light over her shoulder, illuminating the parts strewn across the table. Behind the house, over the water, someone was continuing their celebration, the snaps and cracks loud in the dark.

"Another project," I said, nodding at the telephone, and she laughed.

"You know," she said, "it's always just one thing that needs to be adjusted." She picked up a bracket and examined it, turning it in the light. "But the hardest part is discovering what that one thing *is*."

"I know," I said.

She sighed and looked at me. And then took a closer look, and smiled. "You look wonderful," she said softly. "What's different?"

"Everything," I told her. And it was true. "Everything."

We sat there. Through the living room windows I could hear faint music from next door, soft, drifting love songs. I closed my eyes.

The fireworks kept on across the water, pops followed by laughter and bellowing. "Such a noisy holiday," Mira said. "I hate all the pomp and circumstance, everything blown up into a big deal. I much prefer a nice, quiet celebration."

"We can do that," I said. "Come with me." I got up and found some matches, and she followed me onto the front porch, where we sat on the steps. I shook two sparklers out of the box, handing her one. When it burst into light she smiled, surprised

"Oh," she said, waving it back and forth as the sparks showered down. "It's beautiful."

I lit one for myself and we sat there, watching them in the darkness. "To Independence Day," I said.

"To Independence Day." And then she tipped hers forward, touching mine, and kept it there until they both burned out

chapter twelve

The annual Baptist Church Bazaar was crowded, even at eight A.M. I went with Mira. She pushed her bike over to the church steps, carefully chaining it to the rail while I took a look around.

Most of Colby was there. The church itself was small and white, like something from a picture postcard, and people were milling across its neat green lawn, picking over the displays and tables of junk: mismatched plates, old cash registers, vintage clothing. In the parking lot were the bigger items, like a pop-up camper, an old rowboat with chipped red paint, and the biggest wrought-iron mirror I had ever seen—its glass broken, natu rally—which instantly caught Mira's eye. As soon as the bike was secure she headed right for it, leaving me standing in front of a table stacked with old hamster and bird cages

For the next hour, as I browsed, I was increasingly aware,

again, of how everyone reacted to Mira. I watched as they eyed her, or smirked once she had passed. A few people—Ron from the Quik Stop, the pastor of the church—waved and greeted her. But most of the town seemed to view her as some kind of alien.

"Oh, goodness, look at that," I heard a voice I recognized. "Mira Sparks is already doing her shopping."

I turned around slowly to see Bea Williamson standing there, the Big-Headed Baby on her hip, shaking her head at Mira, who was crouched down, examining a pair of old roller skates.

Maybe it came from facing down Caroline Dawes. Or it could have been building all summer. But suddenly, I felt a fury rise in me toward Bea Williamson and every nasty thing she'd said about Mira in my earshot. It built like a flush, crawling up my neck to make my scalp tingle, so different from my own shame yet feeling the same. I narrowed my eyes at her; she was wearing a gingham sundress and white sandals, her blond hair bouncing as she bent down to deposit the Big-Headed Baby on the grass. When she looked up, her gaze shifted past. She didn't recognize me.

She's got some kind of issue with Mira, Morgan had told me all those weeks ago. *I don't know what it is.*

But there didn't have to be a reason.

I moved to the other side of the table, watching her, and pretended to check the price on a bent hamster wheel.

"I'm surprised she wasn't the first one here," Bea was saying, as the baby toddled past her legs and started around a table covered with plastic placemats. "I half expected her to camp out last night to get the best bargains."

"Oh, Bea," said one of the other women—a clone, in blue and white, same hairstyle. "You're terrible."

"It's just awful," Bea said, fluffing her hair. "Whenever I see her, it practically turns my stomach."

I thought of Caroline again, the way her nose wrinkled when she'd seen me at the Last Chance. And I glanced back at Mira, knowing this wasn't my fight, that if she acted like she didn't care, I should too.

But enough was enough.

I found myself walking around that table, right up to Bea Williamson. I stepped between her and the blue clone, and she stepped back, surprised, then remembered who I was: her eyes went right to my lip ring. The flush was still burning my skin, as I stood there ready to do for Mira what she'd never done for herself.

I took a deep breath, not even sure what words I would say, how I would begin. But I didn't even get a chance.

"Colie?"

It was Mira. She was standing right beside me, with her bike; there was a shiny chrome toaster—priced to sell at four dollars—wedged in the basket. She didn't even seem to notice Bea Williamson and her friend.

"Are you ready to go?" she asked, putting a hand on my arm.

I looked at Bea Williamson, all the words I wanted to say about to spill out. But Mira had already started to push her bike, oblivious, the toaster rattling, and I had to let her lead me away.

We walked together along the road toward the Last Chance, her bike between us. The toaster clanged each time we hit a bump. The rest of her purchases—two old hatboxes, a leaking beanbag chair, and a set of socket wrenches—had been left for Norman to pick up later.

The further we walked, the more what had just happened bothered me, until I couldn't take it anymore.

"Mira," I asked her suddenly, as a car blew past, "how do you *stand* it?"

She looked up at me, dodging a pothole. The toaster clanked. "Stand what?"

"*Being* here," I said, waving a hand at the Last Chance, the Quik Stop, everything. "How can you stand the way they treat you?"

She turned her head. "How do they treat me?" she asked. I wondered if she was joking.

"You know what I mean, Mira." It wasn't like I wanted to start listing things, adding insult to injury. Still, I had to make my point. "The things they say, about your bike, or your clothes. The way they look at you and laugh. I just—I just don't see how you can *take* it, day after day. It's got to hurt so much."

She stopped walking and leaned against the bike, looking at me with those wide, blue eyes, so much like my mother's. "They don't hurt me, Colie," she said. "They never have."

"Mira, come on," I said. "I've spent this whole summer seeing it. I mean, what about Bea Williamson? You can't tell me—"

"No, no," she said, shaking her head, "It's not about Bea Williamson. It's not about anyone. I'm a lucky person, Colie. I'm an artist, I have my health, and I have friends who fill my life and make me happy. I have no complaints."

"But it *has* to hurt you," I said. "You just hide it so well."

"No." And then she smiled at me, as if this wasn't as complicated as I was making it. "Look at me, Colie," she said, gesturing down at her big yellow shirt and leggings, her little purple high-tops. "I've always known who *I* am. I might not work perfectly, or be like them, but that's okay. I know I work in my *own* way."

All this time I'd thought we had everything in common, but I'd been wrong.

I stood there, at the side of the road, and watched as she got on her bike, beginning to pedal slowly downhill toward home. She turned back to wave at me, and then started to coast, the wind picking up behind her. Her hair streamed out and her yellow shirt began to flap wildly, billowing out like crazy wings as, before my eyes, she began to fly.

Around the end of the rush that day, the phone rang and I reached for it, drawing a ticket out of my pocket and my pen from my hair.

"Last Chance," I said. "Can I help you?"

"Is Colie there?"

It was a boy. I glanced back at Norman—the only boy who might logically call me—to see him sitting by the grill reading a book about Salvador Dali and eating french fries.

"This is she," I said. Morgan looked up from her salt shakers.

"Hey," the boy said, relieved. "It's Josh. From last night?"

"Oh, right," I said, leaning back against the coffee machine. "Hi."

"Hi. So, we're getting ready to leave here, but, uh . . ." I could hear noises in the background, people talking and car doors slamming. "But I wondered if maybe I could call you when you got home. I mean, I live in Charlotte too."

"You do?"

"Yeah."

Isabel came down the hallway, her hair up, ready for work. "Take-out order?" she asked Morgan, nodding at me.

"Nope," Morgan whispered. "Boy."

Isabel raised her eyebrows. "Stand up straight."

"He can't see me," I hissed, covering the mouthpiece.

"So we could get together and see a movie, or something. You know, before school starts," Josh continued.

So did Isabel. "Just do it. And don't give him your number, even if he asks for it."

"Isabel," Morgan said.

"Don't," she repeated. "I'm serious."

"That would be great," I said to Josh. "I won't be home till mid-August though, probably."

"Oh, okay," he said. "You want to just give me your number now?" Someone guffawed in the background—another boy— and I heard Josh cup his hand over the receiver.

"Um," I said, and Isabel narrowed her eyes at me, one hand on her hip, "you know, I just got slammed with a bunch of tables. But you can get it from Caroline. She lives right next door."

"She does?" he said. "She didn't tell me that."

I bet she didn't, I thought. Morgan laughed out loud, but Isabel just nodded and got her lunch out of the window.

"Look," I said, "I should go. But call me, okay? In August."

"In August," he said. "I will."

I hung up the phone and looked to Isabel. Norman had put down his book and was watching from the kitchen. Since he'd come back from the bazaar he'd acted strange, ducking his head and not meeting my eyes. I didn't know what his problem was.

"Our Colie," Morgan said proudly. "Look how she's grown."

"You're still slouching," Isabel said.

I smiled at Morgan, who sighed and filled another salt shaker. "Young love," she said. "It makes me really miss Mark."

"Ugh," Isabel said, pouring herself a Coke. "Don't start."

"It was so nice of him to surprise me like that," she said for at least the hundredth time. Mark's unannounced visit had settled her doubts once and for all and left a perpetually dreamy look on her face: Isabel said it could only be love—or gas. "I want to do something to surprise him, you know?"

Isabel just rolled her eyes.

"He's calling me in August," I said, wrapping the phone cord around my wrist.

"Don't accept his first offer for a date," Isabel told me, pulling a magazine out from her stash by the bus pan. "Say you're busy at least once. Twice is better. You call the shots, Colie."

"Right." I wondered how I would handle things when she wasn't around.

I heard the kitchen door slam shut. Norman was gone, his book lying open on the prep table. When I looked outside he was standing by his car, which was packed full with things he'd gotten at the bazaar. Mira's beanbag chair was stuffed in the back seat, a bit of orange fake leather poking out the window.

"Sheesh," Morgan said. "What's going on with Norman?"

Isabel turned another page of her magazine. "He's jealous."

"Of what?"

Isabel looked at me. "What do you think?"

"Not me," I said. "What are you talking about?"

"He likes you. Didn't you see his face when you were talking to him at the fireworks, Colie? It was obvious."

"No," I said. "You're wrong."

"I am never wrong about these things." She glanced outside at Norman, who was now sitting in the front seat of his car, fiddling with the glove box. He slammed it shut; it dropped open. Again. And again.

"Shit!" he yelled.

"See?" Isabel said simply. "He's jealous. He probably had a whole plan for winning your affection. He probably," she said, thinking, "was going to ask you to sit for a portrait."

The portrait. Hot chocolate. "Oh my God," I said, slowly. "Last night. I totally forgot."

"Forgot what?" Morgan said.

"He was going to make me hot chocolate."

"Was he really?" Morgan said, sitting up. "Man, that is good stuff! I am *not* lying to you. He makes it with milk, not water, and then he—"

"Morgan." Isabel put down her magazine.

"Yes?"

"Shut up." She turned to me. "So? What do you think about him?"

"Norman?"

"Duh." Isabel rolled her eyes at me. "Yes. Norman."

I looked outside. He was sitting on the back tailgate of his car now, in his orange T-shirt and black Ray•Ban sunglasses. What did I think of Norman? Yes, he was cute. And he'd been nice to me since my first day in Colby. But he wasn't Josh. On the other hand, he wasn't Chase Mercer, either.

"I don't know," I said. "I like him a lot, but he's just so . . ."

"So what?"

I thought of Josh, with his easy good looks. Then of Norman's uneasy sleep under all those mobiles. "I mean, he's kind of . . . he's not really my type."

"Your type," Morgan said.

Isabel arched her eyebrow. "And what, exactly, is your *type?*"

"You know what I mean," I said. "All that collecting he does. And the sunglasses, and his car . . . I don't know. He's just . . . Norman. You know."

"No," she said, folding her arms. "I don't know."

"He's sweet," I said. "But I don't know if I could ever really go out with him. He's a little out there. You understand *that,* Isabel."

"No, I don't understand that," she said slowly. Morgan put down her salt shaker. "What I do know," Isabel said, gathering steam, "is that when you showed up here all in black, with your friggin' lip pierced and your hair a ratty mess, with more attitude than even *I* have, 'out there' did not even *cover* what I thought of you."

"Isabel," Morgan said.

Isabel held up a hand to stop her. "No," she said. Then she turned back to me. "Look, Colie. Don't let some cute guy make you forget yourself. I never would have encouraged you if I thought you would become like that girl who came in here and called you those things."

"I'm not," I said, hurt.

"Right now, you are." She picked up her magazine again. "Norman is the nicest, sweetest boy I've ever met. If you think he's not good enough for you, you must be better than any of us."

"I didn't say that," I said. I could feel my throat getting tight. Even Morgan wouldn't look at me.

"You didn't have to," Isabel said. "You, of all people, should know that what *isn't* said can hurt the most."

She was right. Mira's words that morning should have taught me something. I took off my apron and balled it up, stuffing it beside the coffee machine. Then I walked out from behind the counter, down the hallway, and locked myself in the bathroom.

I looked at my reflection in the mirror: my new hair, my new eyebrows. My new me. If Isabel was right, I could never forgive myself. Just as my mother vowed never to forget the Fat Years, I could never let myself forget my Years of Shame. If I did, I was no better than Bea Williamson or Caroline Dawes.

I watched Norman from the bathroom window. He was bent over the tailgate, looking for something. He'd never been anything but nice to me.

For the rest of the day, I kept to myself. Isabel was gone by early afternoon, leaving Morgan and me to close together. Norman was in the kitchen finishing up.

All I knew about him was what I'd seen and assumed. So many times I'd sat watching from my room as he lugged strange objects into his apartment: dead fish mounted on plaques, some one's old hockey trophies, a stack of TV trays decorated with the faces of presidents, even an antique waffle iron that was so heavy it got away from him, tumbling down the grass to hit the birdbath with a crash.

Then there were the portraits. That slow, loping way of moving. The sunglasses. And, finally, how I'd hurt him without even trying. When I finally asked Morgan about him, she looked up at me and smiled, as if she'd been waiting for the question.

"Oh, Norman," she said as we sprayed trays with Windex. She glanced back into the kitchen, where he was in the walk-in cooler, examining a box of lemons. "He's a sweetheart."

"He is," I said quietly. If anyone could forgive me for how I'd acted, it was Morgan. "What's his story?"

She put her tray aside and folded her rag, neatly. "Well," she said seriously, "he's had a lot of family trouble. His dad is Big Norm Carswell. He owns that auto dealership, the one with the searchlight, right before you come over the bridge? You've probably seen the commercials. He's got white hair and throws his arms around a lot, screaming about good deals."

"Oh yeah," I said. He was on a lot during wrestling. "I've seen those."

"Yeah," Morgan said. "Anyway, he's a big deal around here. City Council, Tourism Board, all that. Norman's two older brothers have both gone into the business. But Norman . . ."

She trailed off as the cooler door slammed, waiting until Norman emerged with a handful of lemons and went outside.

"Anyway," she went on quietly, "Norman's just not the car salesman type, you know? And a couple of years back, when he started talking about applying to art schools, his dad just freaked. Said he wouldn't pay for it, that it was a waste of time, all that. It was so ridiculous. Norman had already gotten a scholarship; he starts this fall. He's *good,* Colie. You should see his stuff."

I thought of the portrait in Mira's house, and the one I'd seen of Morgan and Isabel.

Norman was on the front stoop now, studying his lemons. He threw one up in the air and caught it.

"So," she continued, pulling down another tray, "it finally got so bad that Norman moved out of his Dad's house. This was, like, last year, when he was seventeen. He packed everything in his car and was just living back here, by the Dumpsters, until Mira told him to come stay with her. It was the same week that cat showed up near dead on her front step. So she took them both in."

"Wow," I said, looking out at Norman, who was still tossing and catching the lemons, studying their falling patterns. "That's amazing. I mean, that his dad would be like that."

"Well, he'd made up his mind about what he wanted Norman to be. He'd assumed too much." She didn't look at me as she said this, but I knew the lesson was there, and I was expected to take it. "And it's so sad, that his dad just doesn't get it," she added. "He never has."

"Get what?" I said, as Norman launched a lemon into the air, keeping it circling with one hand. After a moment he added another, using both hands now.

"Our Norman," Morgan said, as the third lemon was tossed up, and Norman juggled them higher and higher until they blurred into a band of bright yellow. "He's just . . ." And she glanced outside, seeing him, and smiled. "He's special, Colie. That's why you have to be careful. Okay?"

"Okay," I said. She nodded, like we were straight, and went back to work.

Later, when I was done, I went out and found him by the Dumpsters, rummaging through the backseat of his car.

"Hey," I said.

He barely lifted his head. "Hey."

I sat down on the stoop. "What's up?"

"Nothing," he said into the back of the car. He picked up a canvas and leaned it against his bumper, then rested another against it.

"Are those new?" I asked him.

He shook his head. He still wasn't looking at me. "Just some old stuff."

"Look, Norman," I said slowly, knowing this counted, "I'm hoping you'll give me another chance. To get my portrait done."

"I figured you weren't interested."

"I am," I said. "I was stupid. I forgot."

Now he did look up. "You don't have to feel obligated," he said. "I mean, I'm not desperate or anything."

"I know," I said. "I wanted—I *want*—to do it."

He bent over to rearrange the canvases, shoulder blades moving beneath his shirt. "I don't know," he said. "I'm pretty busy these days."

"Oh," I said. I wasn't about to beg; I felt bad enough as it was. "Okay." I stood up and started inside.

I was about to open the back door when he called after me. "I didn't really think about that when I asked you."

I just stood there half in, half out.

"I mean, a portrait is a big commitment," he went on. "It's not just a one-day kind of thing."

"I've got time," I said.

He turned back to the car. I didn't know why this was so important to me, but winning Norman back was suddenly all I wanted. So I stood there, wishing he would turn around.

He didn't. I started back inside, but just as I did I heard him say, very quietly, "Well, okay." I had to strain to hear him. "I mean," he said, sounding resigned, "I guess there's still time."

I felt my shoulders relax and I let out a breath I didn't even know I'd been holding. "Good," I said. "Thanks, Norman."

"But," he told me in a firm voice, "you missed out on the hot chocolate. No second chances on that."

"Okay," I said. "I can take that. When do we start?"

"You still have those sunglasses?" he asked. "The ones I gave you?"

"Yeah."

"Bring them down to my place tonight, around eight, so I can do a sketch. After that we'll work on it there in the evenings, and here, during the day," he said, going around and shutting the tailgate with a bang.

"Here?" I said. "You can do it here?"

"Yeah," he said. "Right here, actually. Under that." And he pointed over my head. "I'll see you tonight."

I turned and saw a sign I'd never noticed before. It was white, painted with red letters. DELIVERIES, it said. And then, under-neath, LAST CHANCE ONLY.

"Okay," I said. "I'll be there."

The first time I'd been in Norman's room I'd thought it was a mess. What I discovered that night was that it was, actually, a carefully ordered universe.

Norman's universe. And in it, everything had a place, from the huge collection of plastic cartoon and action figures on a bookshelf—arranged according to height, like a class picture—to the mannequins he'd had with him the first day we met, which were seated neatly against the walls as if waiting for ap-pointments. There was a workbench lined with baby food jars, each full of something: washers, bolts, brightly colored thumb-tacks, rusty nails, marbles, seashells, tiny plastic doll heads. It looked like he could take anything and make it worthwhile.

The walls were painted white and covered with canvases—some I'd seen before, like the one of Morgan and Isabel, and some I hadn't. Only one other, however, featured the sunglasses theme.

It was a portrait of a man who looked to be in his early twen-ties, leaning against an old-model car. He had a crewcut and wore a white shirt and a tie, black pants and sunglasses, with his arms folded across his chest. Behind him the sky was blue and broad and his head was thrown back with laughter, as if some-one had just cracked the funniest joke in the world. I wondered who he was.

Norman sat me down in an old blue wing-back chair. It

smelled like faded perfume, like roses, and I thought it must be strangely comforting for everything around you to have its own history.

"Okay," he said. "Look right here."

Behind my sunglasses, I wondered how he could tell where I was looking at all. He was sitting across the room on a milk crate, a sketchbook balanced on his lap. Next to him was a coffee can filled with pencils of various colors and sizes that he kept rummaging through, as if he couldn't find exactly what he wanted.

I realized that I was the only thing he was going to be focused on. I was grateful to have something to hide behind.

"Hold your chin up," he said, picking out a pencil and squinting at me. "Not that far. Okay, there. That's good. Stay just like that."

Already my neck was aching. But I didn't budge. Instead, I looked at Norman, almost as if for the first time.

I couldn't say exactly when it happened. Maybe when he bent over, looking up only occasionally, his dark brown eyes moving over and past me, taking me in glance by glance. Or when I watched his hands—which I'd seen flip burgers, capture cats, and cradle eggs, and even held, once—and how they seemed so different now, moving in slow, careful strokes, creating me. The sound of the pencil against paper was the only thing I could hear except for my own breathing. And I felt strange sitting there in front of him. As if he wasn't just Norman Norman, another lazy hippie, but a boy with deep brown eyes, watching me and maybe, if Isabel *had* been right, thinking—

"Don't mess with your lip ring," he said quietly, his eyes still on the sketch pad, his thumb smudging a thick black line.

"I wasn't," I said automatically, embarrassed, as if he could read my mind.

It's just Norman, for God's sake.

He glanced up at me and for one panicked moment I thought I'd said it aloud. This time he didn't look back down at the sketch.

"Something's wrong," he said, still watching me.

"What?" I said, too quickly. "What is it?"

He stood up, putting the sketch pad aside, and crossed the short bit of carpet between us. I felt my stomach jump.

"Hold still," he said, leaning in, and then reached with one hand to tuck a piece of hair behind my ear, his thumb brushing my cheek.

It was just one motion, one movement: it was, really, nothing. But as he went back to his sketch pad, I felt something rush in me, and, behind my sunglasses, closed my eyes. I could see him again in my head, leaning forward, eyes on me, one hand reaching out to touch my face.

"Chin up," he said. "Look right here, Colie."

I took a deep breath, settling myself. This was ridiculous. Mira would have said it was astrological, some crazy moon thing, the kind of celestial pull that drives women into labor and sets werewolves loose on the streets.

Yes, that was it. Just some crazy moon thing.

"Chin up," he said, smudging another line.

"Sorry."

About thirty minutes had passed when behind me, suddenly, the phone rang. And rang. Three times.

"Do you want me to get that?" I asked.

"Nope."

"You sure?"

"Chin *up,* Colie."

The phone rang again. It was the old kind, a rotary, and *loud:* normally, I could hear it two floors up. Another ring, and then Norman's voice crackled over the answering machine.

He was still drawing, not even seeming to notice. There was a beep, and the machine was quiet. I thought whoever had called had hung up. Until I heard it: the sound of someone clearing his throat, as if he was about to say something.

Norman's eyes were focused on the page. The person cleared his throat again, and I watched as Norman lifted the pencil, holding it above the paper, as if waiting for something.

Click. Then a dial tone. Norman went back to work.

We were silent for at least five minutes before I couldn't stand it anymore and asked, "Who was that?"

"What?"

"On the phone. Was that a prank call or something?" We'd gotten tons when the Kiki infomercial hit it big. My mother, for some reason, was also very popular with prisoners. "Does it happen a lot?"

"Chin up," he said, smudging another line. "Eyes right here."

I readjusted my position, jutting out my chin. "Aren't you even going to answer me?"

"No," he said mildly.

"You know, if it's a prank you can get something to trace it,"

I said. It was hard to talk with my chin in the air. "It's not that hard—"

"I know who it is," he said quietly, tilting the sketchbook and pushing his hair out of his face.

"Really? Who?"

No answer.

"Norman."

He put down the sketchbook, dropping his pencil into the coffee can. "Look, Colie," he said, "don't you have some things you'd rather not talk about?"

He didn't say it in a mean way. But something in his tone made me feel like I was a lesser person for even asking.

"Yeah," I said softly. "I do."

"Then you understand, right?" I nodded as he stood up and dropped the sketchbook on the futon. "Okay, we're done here."

"Oh, come on, Norman," I said, knowing now that I had pushed too far. He was so *touchy*. "Don't get mad over that and—"

"No," he said, interrupting me. "I mean, we're *done*. With the sketch." He stretched his arms over his head, his fingers reaching towards the ceiling, a full-body stretch, like Cat Norman. "And we'll start the portrait tomorrow, at work. Okay?"

"Oh," I said. "Okay. But I get to see the sketch, right?"

"Nope."

"But Norman—"

"Good night, Colie."

I knew by now not to push my luck. Instead, I took off my sunglasses and got up, making my way past the mannequins and a stack of stained glass, to the door.

185

When I glanced back, Norman was in the middle of his room, looking up at the protractor mobile. He stood there in the tiny amount of empty space, with all of his objects—bright and colorful—seeming to whirl around him. Now, I'd stepped inside too, and found to my surprise that I liked it there, in Norman's universe, an eclectic solar system that pulled things in, turned them around, and gave them a new life all their own.

We worked together every day, at the Last Chance during the slow parts of the late afternoon, and in the evenings in his room. The portrait had been important to me, but increasingly, so was Norman.

This, of course, was crazy. But ever since that first night, when he'd brushed my hair out of my face, something was different. Maybe not for him. But for me.

It was little things. Like the routine we'd set up whenever we worked, falling into place automatically without even talking. And I'd carved out a space for myself in his room: beside the chair where I posed at night I kept my sunglasses, the water glass he'd given me the first time I said I was thirsty, and the remote for the TV that he swore he never watched except when I was there. There was something nice about having *my* things, and I wondered if he looked at them after I'd gone and thought of me.

I was getting used to his crowded room. He had hung the two sunglasses paintings—Morgan and Isabel, and the man leaning against the car—side by side. I'd sit in my chair, looking through my own lenses as they stared back at me, completed, hanging where my own image would be soon. When I passed through

Mira's back room I found myself examining her portrait, too, reaching out to touch the bumpy surface, wondering what I'd look like when he finished.

The first morning I saw Norman at the Last Chance with paint splattered across his arm I got this strange feeling, some sense of possessiveness, like we shared a secret. I almost wished the sitting would never end.

Sometimes he seemed to be looking at me just for form, as if I was a bowl of apples or a landscape. But there were moments when I'd catch him leaning his head to the side, the paintbrush not even on the canvas, those deep brown eyes really watching me and then—

"Hey, Picasso!" an irritated Isabel would yell from inside the restaurant. "I need some onion rings. Now!"

"All right," Norman would say, putting down his brush. When it got busy he just stuck the canvas in the back of the car, folded up the easel, and went back to flipping burgers while I waited tables. When it slowed down we'd drift back outside and take up our places.

But he refused to show me the painting.

"Bad luck," he said the first time I asked. "You'll see it at the end."

"I want to see it now," I'd whine. This was one of our sticking points; like my mother, I had a hard time waiting for anything.

"Tough." Norman could play hardball when it suited him. "It's a mess now, anyway; it's all still process. The finished product is what matters."

Norman had his secrets. The phone rang almost every night

when we were working, around the same time, 10:15. Norman never answered, and the man on the other end of the line never said a word. He just cleared his throat, as if waiting for someone else to make the first move.

I wanted to grab the phone, forcing the man—who I knew *had* to be Norman's father—to speak. But I couldn't. So I just sat there, night after night, gritting my teeth when it rang.

"Norman," I finally said to him, "*please* answer the phone. Please? For me?"

He shook his head before answering the same way he always did. "Chin up."

When we weren't arguing about the phone, we listened to music. I was—to my horror—almost beginning to appreciate his hippie bands. Or I turned on the TV and flipped through channels, watching shows until Norman vetoed them. One night I came across the Kiki infomercial and introduced Norman to the Buttmaster, FlyKiki inspirational tapes, and Stuffin' for Nothin'. I figured this was more than a fair trade for Phish and the Dead. Norman was intrigued. He even put down his brush to give his full attention to my mother's Super Cal Burn.

"She's really something," he said, as she bent and toned, whipping the studio audience into a frenzy.

"I know," I said. "Sometimes I can't even believe she's my mom."

"Oh, I can," he said easily, his eyes still on the TV. "I see a lot of her in you."

"No way."

"Yep." He picked up the brush, dipping it back into the paint. This was new to me. "Like what?"

"Chin up," he said, and I rolled my eyes. When I did, he continued. "Like your face: it's just like hers, heart-shaped. And the way you hold your hands when you talk, right at the waist. And the way you smile."

I looked at my mother, beaming on national TV. "I don't smile like that," I said.

"But you do," he told me, dabbing at something on the canvas. "Look at her, Colie. That's not fake. On a lot of people it would be, but you can tell she loves what she does. *Loves* it."

I looked back at my mother, listening intently as some woman asked a question about how to get rid of saddlebags. He was right: with my mother, what you saw was what she felt.

"You know," he went on, "I think I knew you for about three weeks before I ever really saw you smile. And then, one day, Morgan said something and you laughed, and I remember thinking it was really cool because it *meant* something. You're not the kind of person who smiles for nothing, Colie. I have to earn *every* one."

I wasn't smiling now. In fact, I was pretty sure my mouth was hanging open *and* I was blushing. Norman ducked back behind the easel and I swallowed, trying to compose myself.

What was happening here? I wasn't even sure it was just in my head anymore.

"Chin up," he said, and I locked my eyes onto his, even as I imagined him leaning closer, tucking the hair behind my ear, again. I'd smile, then. No question. "Chin up."

"It's coming," Mira said to me one morning a few weeks later as we sat eating cereal: me, Grape-Nuts, her, Count Chocula.

My days had narrowed to just work and the portrait, and breakfasts were the one time we still had together.

"What is?"

She picked up a folded newspaper and slid it across the table.

LOCAL MAN GROWS BIGGEST TOMATO ON RECORD, the headline said.

"I don't understand," I said. "Tomatoes?"

"No, no, not that," she said, reaching over and pointing. "This!"

It was a small blurb at the bottom of the page, right beside the weather for the next day. There was a picture of the moon, and the words "*Full lunar eclipse scheduled to occur August fifteenth reaching totality at 12:32 A.M. If the night is clear it should be a perfect time for viewing.*"

"The eclipse," I said. "I forgot all about it."

"How could you?" she said, taking another spoonful of cereal. "Haven't you felt how weird things have been lately? I mean, the cosmos is getting ready to *freak* out. Big changes coming. I can't wait."

Big changes. I thought of Norman, then shook him out of my head. Ridiculous. "It's still a ways away," I said.

She turned to her calendar, flipping up the page. I could see the moon drawn in on the fifteenth, the day circled in purple pen. "Seventeen days and counting. . . ."

"Seventeen days," I repeated. She went back to her paper, searching for the horoscope, happily eating her cereal. To her, change could only be a good thing.

I was thinking of this a few nights later at Norman's. We had the radio on, just enough to hear the music but not the words, and the door open. Out above the water, a half moon was hanging there, big and bright.

"Fourteen days," I said out loud.

"What?" Norman said, poking his head around the canvas.

"The eclipse. It's in fourteen days."

"Oh, yeah," he said. "That's right."

I sat back in the chair, lifting my chin before he asked me to. I was used to it now, the same way I was used to my days revolving around this one thing. I still went to work, and ran on the beach, and made my way through the maze of Mira's notes. But everything seemed like a means to get to this end, the portrait. We'd spent almost a month on it, Norman slowly constructing me on canvas as I memorized each part of him: the arch of his eyebrow, the way his shoulder blade jutted out when he stretched, the smell of turpentine on his skin whenever he crossed the room to adjust my position. I had started to dread the moments when he stopped painting, pausing with the brush in midair, as if at any second he would pronounce it finished and everything would be over.

"I remember the first time I saw a lunar eclipse," he said suddenly, jerking me back to attention. "I was, like, six, and me and my brothers camped out in the backyard to stay up for it. It was the biggest deal."

"Really."

"Yeah." A breeze blew through, spinning the mobiles over my head. "They fell asleep before it even happened, just like my dad predicted, but I remember lying there in my sleeping bag, looking up as the moon just disappeared. And even though I knew what it was, and I was so excited all day waiting for it to happen, I got really scared. Because it doesn't just come right back, you know? There's like this long, long time when it's just *gone*."

I didn't know. I'd never seen one.

"So I ran inside and up to my parents' room and woke up my dad," he went on, dipping the brush into the can of paint thinner and swishing it around. "I was freaking. Crying and everything. And my mom kept saying how she'd known I was too young to camp out and how he should have listened to her—this was before the divorce—and my dad kept telling her to be quiet so he could hear what I was saying, because he couldn't understand me."

He stopped then, and I thought of the voice on the answering machine, clearing his throat. Waiting.

"What were you saying?" I asked him.

"I was saying," Norman said, looking outside, "that they took the moon. They were keeping the moon."

"What did your dad do?"

"He walked me back downstairs and out to the yard, and told me to stop being ridiculous and go to sleep. It wasn't really a big bonding moment." He looked back at the painting in front of him, then at me. "But I will never forget how it felt to lie there and wait for it to come back. Because I wasn't really sure it would. I wanted to believe it as much as I'd always believed the moon could never go away. But I didn't."

"But it did come back," I said. "Eventually."

"It did," he agreed, nodding, looking right at me.

And I never wanted this to end, could have stayed forever in this tiny universe with the radio playing, Norman watching me, and the breeze just blowing through, warm and sweet.

"But it's strange," he went on, "when you've always been told something is true, like the moon *will* come back. You need proof. And while you wait, you feel the entire balance of your world just tipping. It's crazy. But when it's over, and it *does* come back, that's the best, because it's all you want, everything narrows to just *that*. It's this great rush, like for that one second everything's okay with the world again. It's amazing." He looked up at me and smiled and I thought again how I could be happy spending a lot of time, maybe even forever, earning those.

"You'll see what I mean," he said, moving behind the canvas again, out of sight. "You'll see."

chapter thirteen

It was the second week of August, two days before Mira's eclipse, when Morgan came to work with a plan.

"I'm going to Durham to surprise Mark," she announced. She had her hair curled and makeup on, as well as a cute skirt and blouse I didn't recognize. "Will you work for me?"

"That's my skirt," Isabel said.

Morgan glanced down. "You never paid me back the twenty bucks I lent you to buy it. Plus, I'll take good care of it. I promise." Isabel harrumphed, grabbed a water pitcher, and went back out to her tables.

"Can you cover my shifts?" Morgan said to me hopefully. "At least tonight and the morning? I call if I'm going to be longer."

"Sure," I said. The only thing I had going, of course, was the portrait. "No problem."

"I'm just so excited!" she said as Isabel put the pitcher back on the counter. "You know, the schedule is always changing and you can never tell what games are when, but I was reading the newspaper for my horoscope, and I just happened to see on the sports page that the team was in Durham tonight to play the Bulls." The words were tumbling out; I'd never seen her like this. "And ever since he came on the Fourth to see me I've been dying to surprise him back. Plus," she said, leaning closer, "I have this wild idea."

"Yeah?" I said, as Isabel stuck her head between us.

"What wild idea?" she said.

"Well," Morgan said coyly, flipping one of her curls, "I don't know if I should say. . . ."

"You should," Isabel said, her face serious. "Tell me."

"I was just thinking," Morgan said, "that all this wedding stuff has just been so awful for me and Mark. I mean, the stress is ridiculous. I could care less about the ceremony, you know? I just want it to be *done*."

"Wait a second," Isabel said in a low voice.

Morgan didn't hear her. "So I was thinking," she went on, "that if I was in Durham, and so was he, it's only, like, three hours to Dillon from there."

"Dillon?" I said.

"South Carolina," Isabel said flatly.

"They do weddings there," Morgan explained cheerfully. "We can go, do the paperwork, get married the next day and be back for this game against the Bulls."

"Really?" I said. Isabel shot me a look and I quieted down, fast.

"I know what you're gonna say," Morgan said, holding up her hand. "And it is kind of crazy. But Mark is so spontaneous. He'll love it. And if my parents want to throw us a party, great. If not, who cares. We'll be *married*."

She was beaming. But Isabel had That Look.

"Oh, come on," Morgan said, grabbing her hand. "Can't you be happy for me? Just once?"

"I just don't want to see you do something you're going to regret," Isabel said. "Morgan, think about this. Running off and getting married to this guy is—"

"It's not just a *guy*," Morgan said with an easy laugh. "It's *Mark*."

"I know." Isabel frowned. "What I'm saying is, don't go down there with huge expectations, okay? If he's not into the idea, don't freak out. It's really sudden."

"Don't be silly," Morgan said, standing up. "We've been engaged for almost six months. This is the perfect solution. I can't believe I didn't think of it sooner." She picked up her purse.

"Morgan," Isabel said. "Please."

"Don't be such a worrywart." Morgan turned with a jaunty swing of her skirt. "It's all going to be fine, believe me. And the next time you see me, I'll be Mrs. Mark McCormick." She pushed open the door.

"Oh, God," Isabel said softly, and I suddenly realized she was close to tears.

"I'll call you guys!" Morgan yelled as she stepped outside and put on her sunglasses. "Wish me luck, okay?"

"Good luck," I said, and she waved, happier than I'd ever seen her. I started to say something to Isabel. But she had already gone outside and was smoking a cigarette, looking at the sky from under that Last Chance sign as Morgan beeped the horn and drove away.

Someone was shaking me, gently, by the arm.

"Colie."

I opened my eyes, not sure where I was. I looked down and saw the blue chair before recognizing the hand on my arm, flecked with white paint.

Of course. I was at Norman's.

"What time is it?" I said. My mouth was dry and I'd been having a dream that now seemed just out of reach.

"Ten-thirty," Norman said. He was wiping his hands on a rag. "You conked out on me."

"Sorry." I sat up, still groggy. My neck was stiff. "I'll stay awake from now on, I promise."

The phone rang—so damn loud—from behind me, making me jump. Norman stood up and started across the room, back to the easel.

Two rings.

"Norman," I said.

He ignored me, using the rag to wipe a spot on the floor.

Three. Four.

"Norman," I said. I still felt like I was half dreaming. *"Please."*

The machine picked up, the familiar recording repeating itself. "God," I groaned. "I can't *stand* this."

"You want me to answer that?" he said suddenly.

"Yes," I said, even though there was something in his tone that made me hesitate. "But—"

"You're sure?" he asked, cutting me off.

"Norman—"

He was already across the room. His forearm was tense, his fingers white at the tips as they grasped the phone. "Hello?"

I sank down into the cushions. This wasn't my fight, either.

"Yeah. I'm here," he said, lowering his voice. "No. It's okay."

I concentrated on the protractor mobile over my head, trying not to listen. I wondered what his father was saying.

"We've been over this," Norman said in a tired voice. "Nobody is asking you to help me. I'm not expecting it. I did this myself."

I stood up, thinking I'd slip outside until he was finished. But he held up his hand, stopping me, without even turning around.

"I can't believe you," he said, and he laughed this weird, not-funny laugh. "I always thought you would just understand that it was important to me. I really did. I never expected any of this."

I could hear the voice rising on the other end, and Norman closed his eyes.

"Whatever, Dad," he said, and he turned to me. I looked at him and he looked right back, eyes steady, without a canvas or a purpose between us. "You know, you can say it doesn't matter to you all you want. But I'm not the one calling every night, Dad. That's you."

Then he stood there, listening. I couldn't hear anything. And after a minute, he hung up the phone.

"Norman," I said softly. He looked down at his arm, flaking off some paint with one finger. "I'm so sorry. I wasn't—"

"Forget it," he said, shaking his head. "It's okay."

He walked back to the easel and stepped behind the canvas. He looked tired, and I remembered when I'd caught him dreaming. I wondered if it had been his father's face he'd seen then, too.

I sat back down, sliding on my sunglasses. Neither of us spoke.

"It's like," he said suddenly, "I'm the only one of us kids who isn't doing *exactly* what Dad planned. The whole art thing makes him nuts, always has. *His* idea of art is one of those velvet paintings of dogs playing poker."

I smiled. A breeze blew through from the open door, sending the protractors spinning. They clinked against each other and the rulers as Norman watched, just shaking his head.

"I really like this," I said quietly, pointing at the mobile.

"Yeah?" he said. "Geometry was the only subject I ever liked in school, you know, besides art. There's something so even and nice about it. All those theorems and givens. No doubts."

"I know," I said.

"I liked that you could just depend on it to be the same, forever," he said, holding the paintbrush loosely, his eyes on the mobile as it turned and turned overhead. "You could come back to it in a million years and find it just the way you left it." And he looked at me and smiled, and I felt it, all the way to my toes.

"I like that," he said.

It was quiet for a minute, with only the leaves rustling outside. I felt responsible for what had just happened; I wanted things to be even. It wasn't just smiles that you sometimes had to earn.

"Norman."

"Yeah," he said, rubbing his hands over his eyes. It was late. But I had to do something. So I touched my lip ring with my tongue and took a deep breath.

"Remember, when we started, and you asked me if I had anything I didn't want to talk about?"

He wiped off the brush with his shirttail. "Yep."

"Well, I do." I pulled my legs up, sliding off my sunglasses. "What you've seen of me, this summer? It's not really who I am. I mean, it's not who I was."

He raised his eyebrows.

"The thing is," I went on slowly, rubbing my fingers over the worn blue of the chair, "everyone at home hates me."

I expected him to stop me, but he didn't. It was almost scarier that way. I wanted Mira to appear at my elbow, carefully guiding me away just as she had at the bazaar, saving me from whatever would tumble next from my mouth. But I was on my own.

I swallowed. "I used to be really fat," I said, "and we were always moving from place to place until we ended up in Charlotte. And there, someone started a rumor that I slept with this guy when I didn't. I didn't even *know* him. We were just talking, and—"

"Colie."

"No," I said firmly.

Outside, a breeze was blowing again: I could hear Mira's wind chimes. I had to keep going.

"Nothing even happened, but the next day they all called me names and have ever since. That's why I was so mean when you came to pick me up that first day. I wasn't used to anyone being nice to me."

"You don't have to tell me this," he said, very quietly.

"I want to," I said, and my voice was cracking. "You're the only one I've ever wanted to tell."

I still wasn't able to look at him, even as he stepped out from behind the canvas.

"Colie."

I shook my head. "That's the real me, Norman. I mean, not that I did those things, because I didn't. But to them I was always a slut, still a slut."

I choked on this last word. It almost scratched my throat as I forced it out.

"Colie," he said softly. I could feel him watching me; he was that close.

"They didn't care about what it did to me," I said. "It almost killed me."

"But it didn't," he said, and then he reached over and lifted my chin, so I was looking at him. "You knew the truth all along, Colie. That's all that matters. *You* knew."

Now the last year was flooding my mind, all the taunts and terrible things, every ounce of me that had been taken.

Chase Mercer's face, framed in the sweeping arc of a flashlight, already pulling away from me.

Caroline Dawes huddled with her friends across a gym locker room, laughing, mouths open, as I tried to turn my back to change clothes.

The man at the tattoo place leaning in close with the needle toward my lip—this will hurt—as I closed my eyes.

My mother sitting across from me at the dinner table in a brand-new house, pleading for me to tell her what was wrong.

My own angry face reflected back at me as I stared out the train window, pulling into Colby, the last place I wanted to be.

Sitting in Norman's universe, it all began to swirl, faster and faster, and I felt my fingers tightening, holding on.

Let it go, I heard Isabel say in my head. *Let it go.*

The whirling seemed to get louder, and louder, carrying everything with it. And in the center the two of us, sitting so still, rode it out like a storm.

I gripped the chair harder, closing my eyes. Norman was right: I *had* known it all along. And I'd carried that truth near my heart, shielding the most tender part of me.

Let it go, I heard a voice whisper in my head. Maybe it was Isabel again, still teaching. Or my mother, willing her miracles. Mira or Morgan, urging me on. Or Norman, taking that truth like the gift it was. Or maybe it was my own voice, silent all this time, but no longer.

Let it go.

And just like that, I did.

In that instant the swirling seemed to stop, each element falling back into place. I took a deep breath, steadying myself, and opened my eyes, as Norman suddenly stood up and took a step back, as if he'd felt it too.

He was looking at me, and I wondered if my face had changed. If I would look different now, not the same girl he'd been recreating on canvas for so long.

The strangest thing was that I *felt* different. As if something pulled taut for so long had eased back, everything that had been strained settling into place: those forty-five-and-a-half pounds finally gone for good.

"The portrait," I said quickly. I assumed my pose, adjusting my chin, my heart still racing. "We should—"

He glanced across the room. "Colie," he said. "It's done."

"It is?"

"Yep." He turned around and walked over to the easel, dropping his brush into the coffee can. "I put the last touches on about an hour ago."

"Why didn't you wake me up then?"

"I don't know," he said. "You just looked like you were having a good dream."

I got up and stretched, then started over to the canvas. "Okay. Let's see it."

He dodged in front of me—he could be awfully quick, that Norman—and planted himself right in front of the easel. "Hold on," he said.

"Oh, no," I told him. "I have waited and waited. You *promised*."

"I know, I know. And I will show you. I just—I just wanted it to be special"

"Special."

"Yeah," he said. "Look. Let me cook you dinner tomorrow night. And I'll get it all set up and unveil it, make a big deal. So you'll get the full effect."

"Norman," I said, suspicious, "if you are just jerking me around . . ."

"I'm not," he said solemnly. "Cross my heart." And then he did, for good faith. "Dinner and the unveiling. It'll be awesome. Trust me."

"Okay," I said. It was like a date, a real date. "I'll be here."

We said good night, and as I started walking up around the house I remembered my dream. It came to me suddenly, making me stop in midstride.

I'd been at the beach, kissing a boy. I could feel the sun on my face, bright and warm like in the afternoons on the back stoop of the Last Chance. It was a good kiss and I was enjoying it; I pulled my head back and smiled at the boy, who smiled back.

It was Norman.

"Oh, my God," I said. I stopped walking. Cat Norman was on the edge of the porch, licking his paws, and he glanced up at me, startled.

You looked like you were having a good dream, he'd said. And when I'd told him everything, he stayed there, close to me, until we were even.

Suddenly, I saw lights coming down the road. Fast. I heard the car before I saw it, gravel crunching and rattling underneath as it got closer.

I walked around Mira's porch, wondering who would be coming so late. The little house was bright; Isabel was home, sitting out on the front steps with Frank, the guy she'd met on the Fourth of July. I could see the end of her cigarette glowing—she always smoked more when Morgan was away.

The car turned in to the driveway, scattering rocks, its headlights stretching past the trees before flooding the porch. It was the Rabbit. Isabel stood up, shielding her eyes.

"Who *is* that?" I heard Frank say.

The car sped up to the house, swerving slightly, before coming to a sudden, jerking stop. The driver's door opened, and as the light came on, I could see Morgan.

"What happened?" Isabel was already saying, as Morgan ran past up the steps. She'd left the car going, the high beams on, so I could make her out plainly. Her face was red and blotchy and she had her hand over her mouth. She also had something around her neck, something yellow and fuzzy-looking.

Morgan ran through the living room to the bathroom. Isabel dropped her cigarette in the dirt and quickly followed her.

I came a little closer, sticking to our side of the hedge. Frank turned off the car engine and lights, and suddenly everything was much quieter. He stayed outside.

"Morgan!" I could see Isabel through the half-open kitchen window. She was banging on the bathroom door. "Open the door!"

There was no answer. Isabel banged harder.

"Morgan, come on," Isabel said. "You're scaring me."

Isabel, scared. Now that was something I hadn't seen before.

Frank walked inside, hands in his pockets. He stood a re-spectful distance from Isabel, watching, before he said, "Should I—?"

"Go," Isabel said, waving him off. She didn't even look at him. "I'll call you later."

"Right, right." He was already backing away. This was not a place for the weak of heart. I waited until he was gone before moving on to the porch.

"Morgan!" Isabel was yelling now. *"Open this door!"*

No response. I stepped inside.

"This is crazy," Isabel said. She didn't look at me either, but somehow knew I was there. "Tell me what happened," she said to the door. Then, more softly, pleading: *"Morgan."*

"Maybe we should just—" I began. But that was as far as I got.

"You'll be so happy, Isabel," Morgan said from behind the door. Her voice was choked and tight, and I had to listen hard to understand her. "Because you were right. So go ahead and celebrate."

"Just tell me what happened."

The doorknob rattled, taking a second to catch, and then Morgan stepped out. She was in the outfit from that morning, but now it was a wrinkled mess, with one big rip along the front hem of the skirt. She had a bad scrape on her knee. Her eyes were red and swollen, and she clutched a Kleenex in one hand. It was a Hawaiian thing—a lei, I remembered suddenly it was called—hanging around her neck. It was yellow and looked dirty, like it too had been through something big.

"Jesus," Isabel said, looking at her.

"Go on, Isabel," Morgan said, gesturing at her with the Kleenex. "Pat yourself on the back. Do whatever it is you *right* people do."

"What are you talking about?" Isabel said. "Look what you've done to my skirt, for God's sake."

"You were right all along!" Morgan shrieked. "And I know how much you love to be right. How you *live* for it. So do your little dance or whatever. Get it over with."

Isabel raised an eyebrow. "Why won't you tell me what happened?"

"Why should I?" Morgan said. Her voice was high and unbalanced. "You know the whole story, start to finish. You were always so proud of yourself because you had Mark all figured out."

Isabel looked at me. I looked at the floor. We could hear Morgan breathing, fast and jerky, like hysterical people in the movies. I wondered if I should leave.

"Okay," Isabel said in a calm voice. For once, I wished there was music—loud music—playing. "Was there a girl there?"

"Of course there was!" Morgan screamed. "There was a girl living in the hotel with him. And do you know what she was? Do you?"

Isabel sighed. "A stripper?" she asked.

"Yes!" Morgan pointed at her with the Kleenex as if Isabel had won a prize. "And what else?"

"I don't know," Isabel said softly.

"Yes, you do," Morgan snapped. "Come on, Isabel. This is your *game,* baby! Take a guess. A wild guess." I watched the lei move as her chest heaved.

"I don't want to guess," Isabel said. "Why don't you—"

"Oh, no," Morgan said, holding up her hand. "You have to. I'll give you a hint. She was also his"—and she crooked her fingers, making quote marks, and for the first time I noticed the ring, Morgan's touchstone, was gone—*"blank.* Fill it in."

Isabel looked at the floor. I'd never seen her so quiet. "Wife," she said softly.

"Exactly!" Morgan shrieked. "And here's the bonus question. The big enchilada. The brass ring. Ready?"

"Morgan," I said.

"Ready!" Morgan yelled over me. "She was also—*blank* What? What is it?"

Isabel looked out the kitchen window. All I could hear was Morgan breathing.

"Go ahead! She was also—what? What was she, Isabel?"

And then Isabel, in a voice so sad it could break your heart, said, "Pregnant. She was pregnant."

Morgan threw up her hands. "*That's right!* Pregnant! With his kid! You win the couch and the car and the dinette set, Miss Isabel. You win the showcase showdown and all the money. Congratulations!" She was screaming now. *"Congratulations!"* And then she turned around, walked down the hallway to the bedroom and slammed the door so hard it shook the floor beneath my feet.

I looked at Isabel.

"Great," she said. "I win."

We waited an hour for Morgan to come out. Then another.

By two-thirty A.M., when I was nodding off again, Isabel told me to go home.

"There's no point in you sticking around," she said, standing up. "I'll sleep on the couch and she'll be fine in the morning." She looked back at the bedroom door. I could tell she wasn't so sure.

"I can stay," I offered.

"No." She was already stretched out on the couch, reaching up to turn off the light on the end table. "Go. I'll see you tomorrow."

I walked to the door and pushed it open. I could see my bedroom light from the porch, bright and waiting for me.

"Hey, Colie," Isabel called out behind me. The living room was dark now and I couldn't see her.

"Yeah?"

"What were you doing out so late, anyway?"

"Norman and I were finishing the painting," I told her. "It's done."

"Great," she said, yawning.

"He's making me dinner tomorrow," I added softly. "We have, like, a date."

"Really?" Now she sounded more awake. "What time?"

"I don't know," I said. "Dinnertime, I guess." Norman was never one for exactness, exactly.

"Come here first," she said. I could hear her turning over, her voice muffled as she settled in. "And I'll help you get ready."

"You will?"

"Absolutely." Now she was drifting off, her voice soft. "Everything will be fine tomorrow. Just fine."

I shut the door softly and crossed the lawn, cutting through the hedge to Mira's. I passed her bedroom on the way to mine; she'd fallen asleep with the light on, listening to a tape on her headphones, one of which—of course—was missing an earpad. It was still running as I turned her Walkman over and peered down at it, recognizing the tape instantly. I slipped the headphones off and pulled the blanket over her, then lifted them to my own ears, closing my eyes at the sound of my mother's voice.

"I don't believe in failure," she was saying in that confident, breezy way. "Because simply by saying you've failed, you've admitted you attempted. And anyone who attempts is not a failure. Those who truly fail in my eyes are the ones who never try at all. The ones who sit on the couch and whine and moan and wait for the world to change for them."

I smiled. I had heard those words so many times before. And

as I kept listening, I walked to Mira's window and looked at the moon.

It hung brightly in the sky, a bit yellow, ripe and waiting for me. Then I glanced down at the little house. The porch light was on now, and I could see someone sitting on the steps. Someone with her head in her hands, a dirty lei around her neck, sitting under the light of Mira's moon.

"If you try anything," my mother went on, her voice building, "if you try to lose weight, or to improve yourself, or to love, or to make the world a better place, you have already achieved something wonderful, before you even begin. Forget failure. If things don't work out the way you want, hold your head up high and be proud. And try again. And again. And again!"

Try again, I thought, thinking of my night with Norman as I looked down at Morgan, remembering how she'd been so happy that Mark had chosen her. And I wondered where that shiny ring was now.

Try again.

chapter fourteen

The next morning Norman and I were the only ones who showed up for work. Morgan was on the schedule, but I opened alone; luckily it was slow, so I could handle it by myself. I'd thought it might be strange to be with Norman now, but it wasn't. We just ate fat-free potato chips and played Hangman, listening to the radio while he huddled over a grocery list—secretive as ever—planning the Big Dinner. Still, I was glad when two-thirty came and I could close up and go home to find out what was going on.

"It's crazy, Mira," I heard Isabel say as soon as I walked in. "This morning I get up and drive all the way to Starbucks just to get her some of that special snotty coffee she likes so much, and she locks me out! She's been over there crying and playing Patsy Cline ever since. This is bad, Mira. This is *really* bad."

I walked in to the back room and saw Mira sitting at her drafting table, with Isabel on the couch beside her. They were both drinking iced tea with somber looks on their faces. Through the window facing the little house I could hear music. Sad music.

"Her heart is broken," Mira said, sticking her pen in her hair. "You're just going to have to ride it out."

"But I should be there. I've always been there when she was upset like this. I just don't get why this is suddenly all my fault." Isabel looked terrible; her hair was in a sloppy ponytail and she was wearing jeans, a torn red T-shirt, and no makeup whatsoever. She saw me looking and snapped, "I thought I was only going out for a second."

"Fine," I said. I was not going to get on her bad side today.

"She has to blame someone," Mira explained.

"Then blame Mark!" Isabel slammed down her tea glass. "He's the one who cheated on her, married someone else and got her pregnant. All I ever did was—"

"Tell her he was no good. That he was lying to her. That she was going to get hurt," Mira filled in. She shook her head ruefully. "Don't you see, Isabel? She's embarrassed. She's humiliated. And when she looks at you, she knows you were right all along."

"But I didn't want to be right," Isabel protested. "I just didn't want her to get hurt."

"But she did," Mira said. "And until she gets over the shock and comes to her senses and gets *angry*, you just have to keep your distance. The timing is bad too, with the eclipse and all. Everything's out of whack."

Isabel rolled her eyes. "But it's my house, too," she grumbled. "I can't even get to my clothes."

"Give her time," Mira said, looking down at the drafting table. "Or better yet," she said brightly, "give her a card."

"A what?"

"A card!" Mira said, gesturing grandly to the boxes behind her. "There are thousands of ways right here to console her on a loss. Just pick one."

"He's not dead, Mira," I said.

"He should be," Isabel said darkly.

"Go ahead," Mira said cheerfully. "Take one. Take several."

Isabel walked to the shelf and pulled down a box. Mira bounced in her chair, smiling at me.

"So," she said. "Ready for that big date?" I'd told her about it that morning, during our cereal session.

"I guess," I said, and she smiled at me.

Isabel opened up a card and read aloud. " 'I am so sorry to hear of your terrible loss . . . but I know that time, and love, will heal all wounds and that your little friend will live on in your heart forever.' " She looked at Mira, eyebrows raised.

"Dead hamster," Mira explained. "Try another one."

"Okay," Isabel said, opening a second card. "How about . . . 'There comes a time when we all must accept the loss of someone who may not have been truly real but was very real in our hearts. I know this loss affects you in a way some might not understand. But as your friend, I do. And I am so sorry.' "

"Dead soap opera character," Mira said. "That's not right either." She got up and went over to the boxes, rifling through them. "Let's see. How about a dead ex-husband? Or a dead former flame?"

"These are all too nice," Isabel said. "What we need is a good, nasty, empowering card. But nobody makes those."

Mira turned around, took a pen out of her hair, and then jabbed it back in another spot. She was thinking. "*We* could," she said suddenly. "Of course. We'll make a card. How stupid of me!" She went back to her chair, jacked it up, and pulled out a blank piece of sketch paper, folding it in half. "Okay," she said, licking the tip of her pen. "What should it say?" She looked at Isabel.

Isabel looked at me.

"The truth," I said. "It should say the truth."

"Truth," Mira agreed. "So maybe, the front should say something like . . . 'I am sorry for your broken heart.'"

"Perfect," Isabel said.

Mira bent over the card, writing with smooth strokes. Underneath, she drew a heart with a jagged line down the middle. "Okay," she said when she was through. "Now we need the inside. This is the hardest part."

We considered this. Cat Norman walked through, looked at the three of us, and sat down with a wheeze.

"'I am sorry for your broken heart . . .'" Mira read off the front. "but . . ."

"But," Isabel said, "'he was a rotten, cheating rat bastard and you deserve better.'"

"Bingo!" Mira said, whipping another pen out of her hair. "Perfect. And . . ."

"And," I said, "'As your friend, I want you to know that I love you and I know you can get through this.'"

"Excellent." Mira was scribbling madly. "Wonderful. You know, I like this concept—revenge cards. Straight and to the point."

"You should start a new line," I told her as she finished it up with a flourish, then turned it over to sign her name on the back. "Give it a snappy name. Leave the death business and take up empowerment."

Mira looked up. "You're right." She thought for a second. "I know!" she said excitedly, pointing her pen at me. "Heartbreak Diet. That's what I'd call it. I'd make millions."

"You would," I said, smiling at her. "There's even more heartbreak out there than dead people, I bet."

"Okay then," Isabel said, walking over and signing the card in red felt-tip marker before tucking it under her arm. "Wish me luck. I hope this helps."

"Good luck," Mira said.

"Good luck," I said. "Are we still on for later?"

"Later?" Isabel said.

"You said you'd help me get ready," I told her. "For my date."

"Oh, sure," she said. "Just come over in a little while. Give me some time to work this out. Okay?"

"Okay," I said. And I crossed my fingers for both of them as she walked through the yard toward home.

Around eight o'clock, when it was just beginning to get dark, Norman pulled in to the driveway. I stood at my window and watched him unload some groceries; there was celery poking out of one bag. He went around the side of the house, his sunglasses perched on his head, toward his apartment. But just as he turned the corner he looked up at me.

I stepped back. I'd already changed my outfit twice, and finally decided to carry an optional shirt so Isabel could make the final decision.

Mira was parked in front of the television, eating carrot sticks and settling in for an evening of pay-per-view Cage Fighting before the eclipse. She was painting her toenails.

"I'll see you at twelve-fifteen," I told her as I stood behind her chair, watching a wrestler I didn't recognize pull the Lasso Brothers off the sides of the cage by their legs.

She turned around and smiled. "Okay," she said. "Meet me out front."

I picked up my shirt and walked next door, stopping at the hedge when I saw Isabel sitting on the porch, still in the same outfit. She had a beer in her hand.

"The card didn't work?" I said.

She shook her head. "I don't know what to do," she said, running her finger around the mouth of the bottle. "I mean, I've never seen her like this."

"She'll be okay," I said.

"I don't know." The house was lit up and empty. I wondered if Morgan had even come out of the bedroom. "Frank's supposed to be picking me up for a party in fifteen minutes and I don't even think I can leave her."

"Well," I said, holding up my shirt, "you can at least help me get ready. Which one?"

She glanced up. "I don't know, Colie."

"Come on, Isabel."

She put down her beer. "I can't help you, okay? Not tonight. This is—this is just too much."

"But you promised."

"Well," she said, shaking her head, "I'm sorry."

I just stood there. Behind Mira's house I could see the light spilling out from Norman's room. "I can't do it without you," I said. "You know how to do the makeup and my hair, and everything. If it wasn't for you—"

"No," she said. Her voice was tired. "That's not true."

"What am I going to do?" I asked her. "I can't just go like this."

"Of course you can," she said. "You're beautiful, Colie."

"Stop it," I said. She sounded like my mother through all those Fat Years: *You're beautiful. You have such a pretty face.*

"You don't need me." She stood up. "You never did. I didn't do anything but dye your hair and smear on a bunch of make-up. What you were that night at the beach was just *you,* Colie. It was all you. Because for once, you believed in yourself. You believed you were beautiful and so did the rest of the world."

The rest of the world. "No," I said.

"It's true." And she smiled, a sort of sad half smile. "It's like the hidden secret that no one tells you. We can all be beautiful girls, Colie. It's so easy. It's like Dorothy clicking her heels to go home. You could do it all along."

Inside the house I heard a door open, then shut. There was a flash of something that had to be Morgan.

Isabel turned around. She'd seen it too. "Go on," she said. "Have fun, Colie. A first date is a big thing. Enjoy it."

"But—" I said. There was so much I wanted to say, to ask her. Frank was already pulling up, even as Isabel walked to the door and knocked on it again.

"Morgan," she said. She sounded so tired. "Please let me in."

I backed off the porch as Frank got out of the car. And then I slipped back to Mira's and up to my room, to get myself ready for my date and the moon.

Norman was waiting for me with candles lit, a funky quilt spread across the floor, and soft music—the Dead, naturally— playing in the background.

"I've been slaving over this," he said. "I hope you're hungry."

"I am," I said. I'd decided on the first shirt I'd chosen and very little makeup, pulling my hair back the way it had been at the fireworks. I left my lip ring in and told myself to stand up straight, shoulders back. I wanted to believe Isabel, but I had my doubts.

"You look great," Norman said. "Here. Have an appetizer."

For the menu, he had made what he called Moon Food, in honor of the eclipse.

We had small cheese quiches to start. "So you have your cow, the dish and the spoon," he said. Then salad, with blue cheese dressing—which as kids, we all knew came from the moon— and fresh fish from the river on the sound side, the Moonakis (a stretch, he said, but he'd run out of ideas). And finally, Moon Pies for dessert.

"You," I said, pointing the last bit of my Moon Pie at him, "can do wonders with a hot plate."

"It's a gift," he explained. He was on his second Moon Pie—his favorite food, I'd learned.

"I bet," I said. I looked around the room. During all those hours of sitting I had memorized the portraits, the mobiles, the mannequins, everything: I knew them all by heart. The only thing new was in a far corner, covered with a sheet, leaning against the wall.

"You know," I said, "all this time I've been wondering about that painting."

"Which one?"

I pointed to the far wall, where the man was leaning against the car, still laughing. "That one. Is it your dad?"

He nodded. "Yeah."

"He posed for you?"

"No." He ripped open the plastic of another Moon Pie. "I did it from a photograph. It was taken the day he opened his first dealership, the one by the bridge. See that car there? It was the first one he sold."

"Wow," I said, looking at it more closely. "It's really well done, Norman. He must have liked it."

"I don't know," he said quietly. "He's never seen it." He paused. "I didn't want to show it to him, because I knew how he felt about my work. But I've always loved that picture, you know? There's something so cool about capturing a person at a time when they're really just, like, the best they can be. Or have been."

I thought about this, taking in his dad's broad smile.

"That's why I keep it there," he added, brushing crumbs off his lap. "It's the way I want to think of him."

We sat there, not talking, for a few minutes. He ate the Moon Pie; only skinny people can scarf down junk food like that. Finally, I said, "Norman?"

"Yeah?"

"Are you *ever* going to show me the painting?"

"Man," he said. "You are, like, *so* impatient."

"I am not," I said. "I've been waiting forever."

"Okay, okay." He stood up and went over to the corner, picking up the painting and bringing it over to rest against the bright pink belly of one of the mannequins. Then, he handed me a bandana. "Tie that on."

"Why?" I said, but I did it anyway. "Norman, you are way too into ceremony."

"It's important." I could hear him moving around, adjusting things, before he came to sit beside me. "Okay," he said. "Take a look."

I pulled off the blindfold. Beside me, Norman watched me see myself for the first time.

And it *was* me. At least, it was a girl who looked like me. She was sitting on the back stoop of the restaurant, legs crossed and dangling down. She had her head slightly tilted, as if she had just been asked something and was waiting for the right moment to respond, smiling slightly behind the sunglasses that were perched on her nose, barely reflecting part of a blue sky.

The girl was something else, though. Something I hadn't ex
pected. She was beautiful.

Not in the cookie-cutter way of all the faces encircling Isabel's mirror. And not in the easy, almost effortless style of a girl
like Caroline Dawes. This girl who stared back at me, with her
lip ring and her half smile—not quite earned—knew she wasn't
like the others. She knew the secret. And she'd clicked her heels
three times to find her way home.

"Oh, my God," I said to Norman, reaching forward to touch
the painting, which still didn't seem real. My own face, bumpy
and textured beneath my fingers, stared back at me. "Is this how
you see me?"

"Colie." He was right beside me. "That's how you are."

I turned to look at him, studying his face the way, for all those
weeks, he had studied mine. I wanted to remember it, not just
in this moment, but from the whole summer into forever.

"Norman," I said, "It's wonderful."

And then he reached forward, as he had in my mind so many
times, brushing my cheek as he tucked that one piece of hair
behind my ear. This time, he left his hand there.

I thought of so many things as he leaned in to kiss me: that
swirling universe, a million protractors tinkling and finally, that
other girl—me, too—who sat on that back stoop and smiled as
if she didn't even know or care about the sign over her head.

Last Chance.

We were still kissing when I suddenly heard music. Loud,
crazy, boisterous music from the little house.

"What's that?" I said, pulling back and listening.

"Isabel," Norman said into my hair. "Her whole life is high volume."

"No," I said, gently untangling my fingers from his as I got up and walked to the door. "Isabel's out with Frank. The only one there is—"

The music cranked up louder. It was disco, wild and wonderful, beats pounding, a woman's voice climbing and falling over them.

At first I was afraid, I was petrified . . .

"Morgan," I said. "It's Morgan." And when I went out into the yard, by the birdfeeders, I could see her. She danced across the brightly lit kitchen, arms waving over her head, hips shaking.

Either she had gone totally crazy, or Morgan was having a breakthrough.

"Come on," I said to Norman. "Let's go."

The song ended while we crossed the yard. Then it started again. As I pulled the front door open, I had a sudden worry that I wouldn't be able to handle what was going to happen. But by that point, she'd already seen me.

"Colie!" she yelled, waving me inside. "Come on in!"

I stepped over the threshold, with Norman right behind me; he closed his hand around mine. "Morgan?" I said. "What's going on?"

"Norman!" she shrieked, running over to us. "Look at you two! You're so cute together!"

The music was so loud we were all screaming.

"Morgan," I yelled, "are you okay?"

She was bobbing up and down, shaking her head back and forth, but suddenly she stopped. "Come on," she said. "Dance with me."

"Oh, no," I said. "I don't—"

"Please," she said. She put her hand over mine and squeezed, hard. I looked into her eyes and remembered that first day I'd seen her at the Last Chance.

"Morgan," I said.

"I've been going crazy," she said in a rush. "I've been crying for almost twenty-four hours straight and I just didn't know what I was going to do with my life. I mean, nothing is gonna be how I thought anymore. I have to start all over, and that is scaring the *hell* out of me, Colie. And then I realized that there was nothing else I could do tonight. Except this."

The song ended. Then started again.

At first I was afraid, I was petrified . . .

"It's gonna be okay," I said. It was the first time in a long time that I believed it. "It will."

"Come on," she said, and pulled me gently by the hand. "You're my friend, Colie. Dance with me."

I didn't want to do it. But I owed Morgan. So I closed my eyes and let her pull me into the middle of the room, into the music.

I told myself I wouldn't think about that cafeteria at Central Middle. When I danced—and I did—I thought only of that girl sitting on the back stoop of the Last Chance in her sunglasses and her lip ring. She wouldn't be afraid to dance, and neither was I.

The song repeated twice more, and we kept going; me and Morgan shimmying together, laughing, and Norman doing some strange pogo, jumping up and down. *Everyone* looks goofy dancing. I'd just always been so worried about me that I'd never taken the time to look around.

The song had started for the fourth time when Morgan suddenly stopped, her eyes on the door. Norman and I were doing the bump and didn't notice, until he gave me a good knock and sent me flying across the room to the doorway, where I almost crashed into Isabel.

She was standing there, watching us. Frank was holding her hand.

I wondered what she was feeling. Maybe that same strange sadness that I'd felt watching the two of them all those nights from my roof.

Norman and I kept dancing. Isabel was staring at Morgan, and Morgan stared right back.

"I'm sorry," Morgan said loudly. Norman and I stopped; I was out of breath. "It wasn't your fault."

"I never wanted to be right about him," Isabel said. "I was just . . ."

"I know," Morgan said. The song stopped for a second. It was suddenly quiet as we all stood there. She stuck out her hand, palm up. "I know."

Isabel just looked at her, then slid her hand out of Frank's. The music started again. It was the wild finish, the buildup to the end, and Norman grabbed me and twirled me around just as Isabel put her hand in Morgan's, leaned her head back to laugh, and closed her eyes.

"What is this?" Frank said behind me, as Isabel and Morgan bumped against each other, both of them laughing like crazy.

"It's what girls do," I told him. And then Norman and I moved toward them, forming a wild circle, and we rode out the song together.

chapter fifteen

At 12:15, we went to find Mira under her moon.

Norman was holding my hand, with Isabel and Morgan bringing up the rear. Frank had gone home; we figured the dancing had kind of thrown him.

"No big deal," Isabel said. "He was too stuffy anyway."

"I'm going to have to start over," Morgan moaned. "God, I'm going to have to *date* again."

"You'll be fine," Isabel said as we stepped over the hedge. "We'll go someplace new, where there are new men."

"Really," Morgan said. "God, you know, we should. We could go anywhere. And reinvent ourselves, just like in high school."

"Only if you promise to have the same hair that you had in

high school," Isabel said with a snort. "Then we'd meet *all* the men."

"That was a nice cut," Morgan said defensively. "Well, then you have to wear that stupid necklace you always wore, the one with the frog. And those glasses. And—"

"Okay, okay," Isabel said. "You win. We go as we are."

Frog necklace, I was thinking. *Where had I seen—*

Isabel's cousin. The dork with the glasses.

I turned back to look at her. She had her arm linked in Morgan's as they walked, and she was laughing. The blonde hair. The perfect features. The beautiful girl.

So *that* was how she knew.

Now we were under the clear sky, stars scattered above us. And Mira was making her way across the lawn, face upturned to take in the little bit of moon that was left.

When she got to me, I wanted to say something big, something important to mark this occasion. Because maybe it was her, Isabel, Morgan, and Norman who had finally helped me to become. Or maybe, just maybe, I could have done it all along.

But I didn't get the chance. Mira spoke for all of us.

"Okay," she said, tilting her head up to the moon, just a sliver over us. "You can start now."

And as we stood there, watching it be taken bit by bit, I looked across the faces of all these people who meant so much to me. Two months ago, when the train pulled into Colby, the thought that I would be who I was now seemed impossible. As impossible, in fact, as keeping the moon.

But now, as it disappeared, I felt a breeze blow across me.

Norman squeezed my hand, and I could see, as the eclipse reached totality, how he must have been scared all those years ago, wrapped in a sleeping bag in his backyard. Because it is so hard, in any life, to believe in what you can't fully understand.

So I looked down the line at all my friends, knowing I would always remember this. And then I turned my gaze back up to the sky, and put my faith in that moon and its return.